"So how's your new ex-fiancé?"

Startled, Haley met Will's unflinching gaze with one of her own. If she'd learned one thing over the last few years, it was to stand her ground, though there was something about being back in Mule Hollow that seemed to cancel out any time spent away.

She lifted her chin. "I'm fairly certain that he's celebrating at this very moment. After all, he dodged a bullet."

Will raised an eyebrow. "I can understand that perfectly. As I'm certain fiancé number two would agree in kind. Believe me, darling, the day you walked out on me was the best day of my life. I figured it saved me a valley of trouble."

Books by Debra Clopton

Love Inspired

The Trouble with Lacy Brown #318
And Baby Makes Five #346
No Place Like Home #365
Dream a Little Dream #386
Meeting Her Match #402
Operation: Married by Christmas #418

*Mule Hollow

DEBRA CLOPTON

was a 2004 Golden Heart Award finalist in the inspirational category. She makes her home in Texas with her family.

Operation:
Married by Christmas
Debra Clopton

Steeple
Hill®

Published by Steeple Hill Books™

STEEPLE HILL BOOKS

Steeple
Hill®

ISBN-13: 978-0-373-81332-2
ISBN-10:   0-373-81332-5

OPERATION: MARRIED BY CHRISTMAS

Printed in U.S.A.

Trust in the Lord with all your heart and
lean not on your own understanding;
in all your ways acknowledge Him, and
He will make your paths straight.
—*Proverbs* 3:5–6

With a vast amount of admiration and gratitude,
this book is dedicated to Joan Marlow Golan,
Executive Editor for Steeple Hill Books.
Thank you for all you do, but most of all thank you
for believing in my first book and buying it.
You made my dream come true!

Chapter One

She was so close—only five miles from a warm bed and sweet dreams.

She needed oblivion…. She did not need *this!*

Bleary-eyed and road-weary, Haley Bell Thornton peered through the window of her BMW Roadster and frowned at the cowboy blocking her path. With the stiff-armed motion of a traffic cop he signaled for her to halt.

Behind him stood a group of men hunched over the open hood of a truck that was connected to a cattle trailer. A cattle trailer that was completely blocking the road to Mule Hollow.

Haley was not a happy camper as the tall, lean cowboy strode toward her. Collar flipped up around his chin, he'd pulled his hat low over his eyes to hamper the frigid November wind. Haley groaned wearily when halfway to her car the man halted and responded to something one of the cowboys called out to him. "Come on," Haley said, snippy from fatigue as she rested her forehead against the steering wheel. She needed sleep and this delay was not in her plan.

Yeah, right, what plan was that?

Haley closed her eyes. As the bride who had backed out of a church chapel, dropped her bouquet on the sidewalk, hopped in her car and sped away with her veil flapping in the wind, Haley couldn't exactly say she had a plan.

Lost her marbles—now that she could say.

As could everyone else who'd watched her walk out on the groom who had more money than Bill Gates… Okay, so that was stretching things a bit, but in the realm of the ultra-wealthy, Lincoln Billings could hold his own.

She'd warned him, though. Been up-front with him. He'd known full well she didn't love him. Known she'd attempted to walk the aisle two times prior and had yet to make it to the altar.

But that had only fueled Linc's competitive spirit, and Haley had gotten caught up in his game. She'd let him talk her into attempting the notorious wedding walk once more.

Attempt being the key word. Poor Linc, he'd so believed his charm and his millions would be the antidote to her problem.... At least it was only his ego she'd damaged and not his heart.

A knuckle rapping on her window brought Haley out of her daze. She blinked and straightened in her seat. Oh, how she needed to get to Grandpa Applegate's place. She needed to crawl into a warm bed and pull her grandma's quilt over her head. She just needed to block out the world for a few days and rest.

But she was in Texas cattle country, and she had forgotten that it unfortunately came with unique problems. Like broken-down cattle trailers and shoulderless roads that rendered low-to-the-road sports cars, like hers, useless. Grumpier by the moment, she pressed the button and lowered the window just a crack. Instantly, her car interior chilled and her eyes stung from the bite of the near-freezing wind that whisked through the slight opening.

"I need to get by here. Would you move that thing?" she snapped, giving the cowboy only a quick glance before returning her glare to the no-good trailer.

"Well, ma'am," he drawled. "I thought that might be your plan. I mean, you *are* heading north. But as you can see the truck has stalled. And as you can also see, I'm just a mere man."

The instant she heard his voice, Haley's gaze whipped from the trailer to his face…or at least she tried to see his face. He was standing too close, and she had to scoot down and angle her head to the side so her car roof didn't cut him off from sight. Even at this odd angle his features were shadowed beneath his black Stetson. But Haley knew him. She would have recognized Will Sutton's voice anywhere.

Will's slow drawl always had done funny things to her heart. Rich and silky, it had never failed to connect with her.

Will Sutton! She snapped out of her stunned surprise and bolted upward so fast she banged her head on the roof. What was he doing back in Mule Hollow?

Her gaze dropped to her gown and she wanted to shrink into the floorboard of her car. Oh, why hadn't she taken the time to change? Only a crazy woman walked out of her wedding and drove eighteen hours in her wedding dress.

"Haley?" Her name whooshed from his lips as if he couldn't believe what he was seeing.

Haley cringed and ducked her chin; a loose curl slapped her in the forehead and she closed her eyes. She looked like roadkill. A woman wasn't supposed to look this way when she met—

"Haley, is that you?"

Okay, so she couldn't very well remain hidden behind a single golden curl and a clear sheet of glass. She opened her eyes and took a deep breath. Maybe, just maybe, he wouldn't realize she was wearing a wedding dress. After all, it was a simple, elegant Vera Wang sheath. A guy would just look at it and think: white silk dress.

Right?

Her mouth was as dry as dirt and her insides wobbly as she reluctantly let the window down farther. He had bent forward so that he could see her better. Warily, she met his disbelieving gaze. The man had the most gorgeous brown eyes. Soulful and bottomless, with gold flecks that sparkled when the sun hit them just right.

Get over it, Haley! The man hates you. And you're not too peachy about him, either, remember?

"Will, hello," she gasped. As a real-estate agent for one of the most prestigious agencies in West Hollywood, she was known for her lightning-quick response in any situation. But with the way her throat closed off now, the only lightning she could hope for was a bolt to strike and put her out of her misery.

Will blinked twice, straightened to his full six foot three inches and let the awkward moment stretch. Endlessly.

Haley swallowed again. Will Sutton was still the best-looking man she'd ever seen.

He was also the first man she'd ever left at the altar. The first man to break her heart. And the last.

"Well, what do you know?" he drawled finally. "Haley Bell Thornton has come home at last."

His patronizing tone stung and riled her at the same time. "It's a free country," she snapped. She had a thing about condescension.

The laugh that escaped his perfect lips was about as disdainful and condescending as it could get. "If it were that free, I'd think you'd come see Applegate every once in a while."

She bristled against words that cut to the quick. She had neglected her grandpa. "I hardly think what I do is any of your business." Tension sparked between them sharper than the cutting wind.

"On that count you'd be right, Haley." His eyes narrowed.

"Look. Are you going to move that thing?" She lifted her chin for good measure while her traitorous heart did a lunge-and-dive maneuver against her ribs. Without warning, her eyes betrayed her and dropped to his hand. But the hand, along with the telltale ring finger, was buried in the pocket of his coat. Astounded at herself, she immediately looked away, hoping he hadn't seen.

No such luck.

"I'm not married, Haley. Never have been."

Again her tongue failed her. What was she supposed to say to that?

"You, on the other hand," he drawled, cocking his head to the side to get a better look at her. "You look as though you've been playing dress-up again." His condemning gaze took in her dress then met her eyes straight on. "What is this, the fourth time?"

"Third," she gritted from between flattened lips. Had she actually *liked* this man at one time?

He pulled his hands from his pockets, holding them up in a "no foul" gesture. "Don't look at me. I moved back here three months ago, and the rumor mill started churning out Haley Bell reports without me so much as opening my mouth."

Ohhhh!

"You," he continued, despite her warning glare, "have really done yourself proud."

That did it! What did he know? Who did he think he was? "Look, I'd just love to sit here and reminisce, but it is cold and I'm tired and I need to get to my grandpa Applegate's."

"Well, let me put a fire under the boys, then. We certainly wouldn't want *you* to be the one left standing out in the cold."

Before she could say anything, he spun on his boot heel and strode back to the truck. He spoke to the guys, who immediately looked her way as he left them and stalked around to the far side of the trailer. Through its bars she could see another truck, and to her dismay Will climbed into it and drove off toward town—leaving her trapped with nothing to do but sit and wait!

Haley fumed as she watched him disappear into the distance.

Payback was the pits.

Chapter Two

A few miles down the road, Will yanked his truck to a stop and stared out across the expanse of ranch land on the edge of town.

Haley Bell Thornton was back.

And he had to pretend it didn't matter to him. Had to act as if he'd never loved her. As if watching her walk out of that church, leaving him standing alone at the altar ten years ago, hadn't torn his heart out.

Will had always been a what-you-see-is-what-you-get kind of man. Pretending didn't work for him, which accounted for his behavior just now. He'd let his guard down—*what guard?* He'd been so shocked when he'd realized Haley was sitting right there in front of him that he'd had no guard. Just pure reaction. And he'd reacted badly.

He was not normally a rude man. His faith in God's plan for his life had been rocked to its very core after Haley had left him, but he'd learned to accept it and not blame God for it.

Haley was here, and he would simply deal with it. He wouldn't allow himself to act like a child again. He'd make certain that the next encounter with Haley would be different. It had to be if he was going to come out of this with his self-esteem—not to mention his heart—intact. After all, Will was only a man.

Not that he would have to see her again while she was here. With Christmas coming he had plenty to do to keep busy. He had enough work lined up to keep him burning the midnight oil for the next six weeks, designing the custom gates and steel signs he was known for. Business was brisk. It never failed to strike him how blessed he was to be making a living doing something he loved. The demand for a custom Sutton gate was high. His western views decorated ranch entryways all over the world, a source of pure satisfaction for Will.

Through hard work and endless hours, he'd built a name for himself. All he had to do now was bury himself in his work the way he'd been doing for years and make it through the week. Only a week. Haley had proven she hated Mule Hollow, Texas. There was no way she would last here longer than one week.

If she lasted that long.

As far as he could tell, she'd achieved exactly what she longed for when she'd chosen Beverly Hills over him. Applegate had mentioned that she'd just sold her first multimillion-dollar mansion to a big Hollywood star. The commissions off sales of that magnitude would be hard for a person like Haley to stay away from. And a California real-estate agent couldn't make sales from four states away.

Will didn't know what brought Haley home, but there was no way he'd let his guard down while she was here. No way he'd take a chance at being left standing in the dust of her departure this go-round.

There was only so much a heart could take. His designs might be made of steel, but his heart was not.

Trudging up the steps to her grandpa's— who had gone by plain, ol' Applegate for as long as she could remember—Haley tripped on the hem of her dress. Yanking it up to her knees, she stomped to the door and twisted the doorknob as if it were Will Sutton's neck. At this time of morning, Applegate would be in town playing checkers with his buddy Stanley. Rain or shine they passed the mornings away with daily checker games at Sam's Diner. Poor Sam; Haley could only imagine what he had to put up with from those two constantly being underfoot.

Haley walked into her grandpa's home, a little perturbed at him for not locking his door. He never locked his doors, didn't think there was a need for such a thing in Mule Hollow. That was something she was going to have to speak to him about. Things changed. The world was not the place it used to be.

Glancing around the tidy living space, she made her way directly toward the back of the house and the spare bedroom. The big, warm bed sat exactly where it always had across from the windows. Not much had changed in the years since she'd been here. It still looked as if her grandmother had only left the house briefly and would be back momentarily. Nostalgia filled her as her gaze rested on a picture of her grandparents on their wedding day. It hung on the hall wall, and she glanced from the doorway to admire it before entering the guest bedroom. How her grandmother had put up with Applegate for almost fifty years had been a mystery to everyone. The thought made Haley smile. The two had a happy marriage up until Birdie had passed away six years ago. Haley sighed, walked to the big bed and pulled the coverlet back. Weary beyond description, she slipped off her shoes and dropped fully clothed onto the bed. Her grandparents had possessed something that eluded Haley.

Oh, forget it. She was too tired to think about anything right now. She needed sleep. She'd been on the road since two o'clock the day before, and the bed was calling her name. She pulled the covers over her head, sighing as her bones relaxed into the soft mattress. With any luck she hoped for at least a couple of hours' sleep before Applegate came home and found her.

She was going to need it.

Because there was no escaping the fact that Applegate would put her through the wringer with questions and unwanted advice once he found her. He was not known for his patience. It was a quality she'd inherited.

Closing her eyes, Haley's thoughts immediately went back to Will, and she groaned into the heavy quilt. What were the odds that he would be the first person she'd see upon coming home? The man was supposed to be living in the Dallas area building malls or something.

This weird coincidence was just one more of the odd things that had been happening to her over the last month. Things that some might think random, but added together ended up bringing Haley home—after she walked out on yet another wedding. And probably did irreparable damage to her hard-won reputation as one of *the* go-to real-state agents in Beverly Hills.

Sleep wrapped around Haley's thoughts, and despite herself she fell asleep with a picture of Will in her mind and the question she couldn't answer.

Why had she come home? Really?

She had a great life…. She had a life she'd worked hard for…. A life she'd dreamed of…

Why had she walked out on it and come back?

Haley woke to the sound of hushed voices and multiple sets of footsteps clomping down the wood floor of the hallway.

She'd just pushed her head out from beneath the covers when a crowd appeared in the open doorway. Her grandpa stood in the front, as tall and lean as a beanpole. Stanley stood beside him, shorter and softer around the middle. They were flanked by Esther Mae Wilcox and Norma Sue Jenkins. All of them were gaping at her with open mouths and wide eyes.

Oh boy, there was nothing in the world like the puppy in a pet store feeling to snap a person out of a groggy fog.

Haley sat up and gaped right back.

Instantly, Applegate's wrinkles lifted into a grin. "Haley Bell, youngin, we heard you'd snuck yourself into town and we come to see about-cha. To see if it was true."

As usual he spoke louder than needed because his hearing was so bad. He'd worked thirty years in the oil field as a driller before semiretiring as a rancher. The loud machines had ruined his hearing early in life, but he wasn't fond of his hearing aids and didn't always turn them on. Now, in an unusual show of affection, he bent down and engulfed Haley in a hug.

As Haley returned his hug, she realized that though there was still strength in his bony frame, he'd grown thinner, if that was possible. She was overcome with shame for all the long-distance phone calls and excuses for not being able to come home for a visit. She was a slug.

His thinness reminded her of their last phone call, the call that had alarmed her enough to make her finally come home. He'd mentioned a bad report from the doctor, but he refused to share details about it. That had been the most important thing, but one of many that had sealed her spur-of-the-moment decision to head her car this direction as she sped out of the chapel parking lot. She still wasn't certain about anything else, but she was glad that she'd come if for no other reason than to see about her grandpa. Will was right. She'd been selfish.

"I've missed you too, Grandpa," she said, blinking back tears, overwhelmed by how much. Fighting to control her emotions she smiled and nodded toward the others. "But, um, what's with the show?" She lifted her eyebrow when her audience crowded closer then swamped her with enthusiastic hugs. She couldn't get a word in as she was smothered, squeezed, cooed and clucked over. Her cheeks were even pinched by Esther Mae, making Haley feel six years old all over again.

After a moment they stepped back and studied her again—as if they couldn't believe she was really here. Haley studied them, too, knowing that to them she'd never grown up. She'd always been their little Haley Bell and it was obvious that she'd been right all those years ago to realize that some things would never change.

To them she would always be the adorable little girl with the Shirley Temple hair who tripped over her shoelaces and knocked over the buffet table at church socials. Among a host of other mishaps that she'd never been able to live down while living in Mule Hollow.

"We were all having coffee at Sam's when Nate Talbert came in with the news that you'd come to town." Robust in body and soul, Norma Sue beamed the broad smile Haley remembered so well.

Haley leaned her head to the side. "Who's Nate Talbert?"

"Nate's trailer was blocking the road," Esther Mae offered, patting her short red hair. It had gotten flattened on one side during all the hugging. Haley noticed instantly that Esther Mae had had a makeover since the last time Haley had seen her. There was no forgetting the long hair Esther Mae had always teased and sprayed into a mountain on top of her head. There had always been the threat of a rock slide with the way she bobbed her head as she spoke. Now it was shorter, more-up-to-date and saucy—like Esther Mae herself.

"Nate said you ran poor Will off, surprising him like that," Stanley boomed. He, too, had a hearing problem.

Ran him off!

Haley's shocked gaze met Applegate's just as his bushy brows suddenly dipped together.

"Youngin, what in the world do you have on?"

"Oh!" Haley gasped as everyone's attention dropped to the rumpled wedding dress she still wore. She cringed and wanted to crawl under the bed. Why, oh why, hadn't she taken the time to change?

Yes, she'd been dead on her feet, but this was really getting ridiculous. This was going to be one more Haley Bell tale to add to her already notorious dossier.... "Um, well—"

"Look at that, Norma Sue. That is a wedding dress!" Esther Mae exclaimed. "Haley Bell's been at it again. Again—"

"Esther Mae, get a hold of yourself!"

Norma Sue barked, rendering the room silent as she placed her hands on her ample hips and studied Haley. "*Is* that a wedding dress?"

"Yes." The word came out in a squeak as Haley dropped another year from six to five years old. This was not good. A month ago she had mentioned to Applegate that she was thinking about getting married. She was getting older, after all. But he'd gotten so agitated by the news that she hadn't called him back to say she'd decided to go through with the wedding rather than wait. After all, she was a grown woman. It had been ten years and she'd grown up. She didn't need him or the town telling her once more what she should and shouldn't do.

"You didn't go through with it, did ya?" Applegate asked, his face drooping into a scowl.

"No, Grandpa, once again I didn't go through with it." To her surprise a collective sigh passed from everyone in the room. Of course, she realized suddenly by their reactions, Applegate had shared with everyone that she'd been contemplating another wedding. One that didn't include love.

"I'm glad ya come to yor senses and didn't go through with it," he said, nodding his head. "Haley Bell, darlin', you gotta love the one you marry and that's all thar is to it."

"That's right," Stanley added. "Even if it takes lookin' foolish a time or two fore ya know where yor heart belongs."

Haley bit her lip at that one. There was nothing like the brutal honesty a girl got from the ones who'd practically raised her. From the ones who might not ever let her grow up, but loved her in their own smothering way.

She sighed, gazing from face to face…. *Welcome home, Haley. Welcome home.*

Will stared at the eight-foot sheet of steel that was the canvas for his art. Intently he studied the scene he'd just finished chalking out. It was a small herd of cattle grazing beneath several oak trees. Once he cut it out with his plasma cutter, the welding torch he used, he would mount it in a frame of steel bars. After grinding the edges and adding a black powder coating, it would become an entrance gate for a wealthy ranch owner out of Wyoming.

"So, can you do it?"

Will turned back to Norma Sue and Esther Mae waiting impatiently for an answer. They'd arrived only moments before beaming with excitement. He'd known he was in for it the instant he saw Norma Sue's truck winding up his drive. This day had started out on the wrong foot with his early morning run-in with Haley and now this….

"Norma Sue, I'd like to help with the Christmas production, but like I said, I have commitments."

"Well, it's really not a lot that we need," Esther Mae whined, her feelings obviously hurt as she glanced from him to her cohort. "Tell him, Norma."

Norma Sue cleared her throat. "Right. Will, all we need is some simple welding. Mind you, it needs to look good, and you are the best there is when it comes to welding."

"Oh, yes. That's the truth," Esther Mae chimed in, nodding. "And we need just a little, teeny bit of drawing, too." She waved toward the chalk scene. "And everybody knows you can draw anything."

Will was no greenhorn, and he knew these two were only getting started with their persuasive tactics. He didn't have time; he was telling the truth. For despite the snow job, he had great respect for the two ladies in front of him and felt guilty turning them down. After all, he'd moved back to Mule Hollow because he'd read about the way the ladies and their friends were trying to keep their town on the map, and he admired their efforts.

He'd also felt an obligation to come home.. He had a business that could thrive from any locale, so it just didn't feel right to stay away any longer. He figured the least he could do was give back to the community that had given him so much growing up. In truth, he'd missed Mule Hollow. He'd decided it was high time to put the ghost of his past behind him, and that could only be done if he came back to Mule Hollow and faced at least part of it.

He studied their beaming faces. "Well, maybe I could find some extra time—"

"That's our boy!" Norma Sue exclaimed and slapped him on the back so hard he choked. "We knew you'd come through for us."

His eyes watered as he struggled for air, nodding along with them. He was a wimp and they knew it. Still, he couldn't help smiling back at them…after he finally stopped choking.

On her second morning in Mule Hollow, Haley was awakened at sunup by Applegate.

He was on his way to Sam's but wanted her to come to the diner around nine for breakfast with him. Sam's Diner had been the mainstay of the community for as long as she could remember. She agreed to breakfast without a fight. Sam's eggs were to die for and his coffee... Well, there wasn't anything like Sam's coffee.

At eight o'clock she called her office and spoke to her assistant. Sugar relayed the consensus of the office—it was exactly what Haley had believed it would be. "Girl, if you're crazy enough to walk out on a free ride like Lincoln Billings," Sugar said, "then you've obviously gone off the deep end and need a break. And a therapist!"

Financially, Haley could afford the time off, but career-wise she felt vulnerable. She imagined that her employers were wondering if the stress of working with their high-end clientele was getting to her. Sure, they were being cooperative, but she knew they wouldn't wait long for her to return. Haley knew firsthand how competitive the market was. They had to keep up or lose out. If she couldn't cut it, they'd be forced to find someone who could.

Haley pushed the pressure aside and

focused on taking it one day at a time. She'd been working at the speed of light for so long it was going to be hard for her to slow down, even for a little while. But something deep inside of her was telling Haley she had to back off. And she was just tired enough to listen.

Promptly at nine she drove into town and was shocked at what she saw. Mule Hollow had changed so dramatically that she was rendered speechless. Main Street had always been a straight shot of wood-fronted buildings dissected by a county road with a few adjacent buildings and anchored on the far end by the majestic turreted home of Adela Ledbetter. It had always had the look of an old western town. When one was approaching Mule Hollow, it stood out on the horizon like a weathered plank fence with a few broken boards. When she'd left, most buildings had been vacant and so worn that it was depressing. Today, her first glimpse of the rainbow of color was so vivid she gasped with shock.

There was the bright pink building she'd read about in Molly Popp's weekly newspaper column—it still amazed her that her home had a syndicated weekly column written about it. Not only did she read it, but it was sometimes breakroom talk at the office. Haley stared at the pink hair salon surrounded by all of the other colorfully painted buildings. It had taken a newcomer, Lacy Brown, to help liven up Mule Hollow. Her building, the one that had sparked the change, stood out like a flamingo in a spring bouquet. Haley was floored and saddened by the new upbeat appearance....

Not saddened that such a wonderful thing had happened, but that she'd been in such a hurry to leave the dying town behind ten years earlier that she hadn't seen any value in it. It saddened her that it took an outsider to see the potential. It saddened her to realize that she hadn't stuck around to help revitalize her home town. Guilt at her selfishness began to leak in around the corners of the memory. Then again, she was the town's little Haley Bell, who would have listened to her if she'd suggested that they paint the town blue and pink?

No one would have. They would have patted her on the head and had a good chuckle.

Cutting the thought off, she turned into the parking space in front of Sam's Diner.

She had gotten where she was in her career by adhering to a strict set of rules. She didn't look back…. At least she tried not to look back. Still, memories stole up on her at times, forcing her to push them away in order to focus on achieving her new goals. Looking back stole energy away from her forward progress, from achieving her future. Looking back was not productive. And Haley was very productive.

Aside from that, she knew firsthand that sometimes looking back hurt far too much.

Then why had she come home?

That question was ridiculous. She'd come to see her grandpa. Hadn't she? She'd come home to rest. Or was she searching for something? Something that had caused this restlessness that had stolen over her in the last few months.

She was almost to the steps when she heard someone call her name. Spinning around, she saw Brady Cannon striding across the street. Brady had been ahead of her in school and loved to pick on her growing up. He was now the sheriff of the town and had recently married. Applegate said he was as happy as a rabbit in a carrot patch. Looking at him now, Haley believed it.

"I heard you were in town, Haley Bell, Haley Bell," he said, smiling.

Despite how she'd hated the teasing "Haley Bell" chant growing up, Haley laughed as he swept her into a bear hug. It seemed like a thousand years since she'd heard the familiar chant that he and his friends—including Will Sutton—used as they followed her around tugging on her pigtails. Nothing had given them more pleasure than to tease her when she did something they thought was funny.

"How are you?" he continued as he let her loose and stared down at her.

Brady was one of the tallest men she'd ever met. A giant of a guy who had always wanted to escape Mule Hollow the same way she did. He'd done it, too, and now he was back. She wondered what had changed his mind and brought him back. She wanted to ask him, but now wasn't the time.

"I'm doing okay," she said, tipping her head up to see his face.

"Okay? From what Applegate tells us, you're setting the world on fire out there in the land of the rich and famous. Just like you dreamed."

"Yeah, well, it's a living."

He studied her. "Is that a little disenchantment I hear in that reply?"

What could she say to that? "Maybe. Not sure," she admitted. "But whatever you do, please don't tell Applegate or he'll start a campaign to get me to move back home."

"And would that be so bad?"

She shrugged. "I don't know." She glanced down the street. "Things certainly have changed since I left."

Brady smiled. "Things are looking up for our little metropolis."

He looked so happy. Haley studied him. "Sheriff, I believe marriage agrees with you."

"God has really blessed me, Haley. I don't regret being a cop in Houston, but it took coming back to Mule Hollow for me to find my heart."

"Are you sure you're the same guy who used to torment me and dream of leaving Mule Hollow behind?"

He grinned. "Do I sound sappy?"

"Oh, yeah. But nice. It's got to be a great feeling. Not that I would know…" Her voice trailed off, letting the rest go.

"It's obvious you made the right decision calling off another wedding."

Haley frowned. "What?"

Brady's eyes twinkled. "Yes, I know about it. You know how fast word spreads. What I'm saying is, if you'd loved the guy like I love Dottie then you'd understand the sappiness. And you'd be on your honeymoon right now rather than standing here in the middle of Mule Hollow talking to me."

"True. I guess I just can't help wondering if there is something wrong with me. You know? Three tries and I'm still running. Needless to say, I'm giving up on weddings."

Brady surprised her by giving her a quick hug. "Don't do that. Life isn't a straight road, Haley. You might be surprised at where its twists and turns may lead you. Believe it or not, God is in control. Come on inside. I didn't mean to keep you away from your breakfast."

"I have missed Sam's eggs," she admitted.

"They've only gotten better over the years. He's pretty sappy himself these days since he and Adela tied the knot. It's not Adela Ledbetter anymore, but finally Adela Greene."

"I think that is so wonderful after all these years," Haley said as he held the swinging door open for her and she stepped inside. There was no place on earth that smelled like Sam's combination of coffee, eggs and the scent of old pine wood floors. Memories crashed though Haley's mind in such a vivid wave that she came to a dead halt.

As did every conversation in the diner.

Chapter Three

Okay, so why did she feel like the prodigal daughter? The question drummed through Haley's head as every eye in Sam's gave her the once-over. First up, then down, painstakingly slow, she felt the gazes moving over her. Of course, she'd expected it. She knew she looked out of place in her black silk pantsuit and her four-inch heels. She was, to say the least, overdressed. But she only had what was in her suitcase. A suitcase packed with honeymoon outfits.... And since she and Lincoln had been headed for the Riviera, her outfits were not exactly what you would classify as everyday Mule Hollow attire.

She wasn't a blusher. Instead, she lifted her chin, feeling as if someone had hit the pause button on the movie of her life.

She saw cowboys she'd grown up with and a few faces she'd never seen before smiling at her. Not surprising was the fact that even though she didn't know all the faces, it was clear from their expressions that they knew exactly who she was. It wasn't all cowboys, either. There were women in the mix looking her up and down, too. There were Esther Mae and Norma Sue grinning like possums. And their buddy, sweet Adela with her shining blue eyes and white wispy hair, smiling kindly as if she knew what thin ice Haley was skating on. Because Mule Hollow was too small to have its own school they'd always shared a centrally located school about twenty miles away with two other small communities. Looking around the room, she was startled to see cowboys she recognized. Obviously the cowboy way had had more of a pull on them than the girls, because she didn't recognize any of the women. No wonder Norma Sue and the others had resorted to advertising for women to move to town.

And they were smiling, too. As if they were more than glad to be living and breathing Mule Hollow air. As if they could live here for the rest of their lives.

Suddenly, as if the pause button had been released, the diner erupted into sound and movement. Yet Haley's mind continued to move in slow motion as everyone started clapping and shouting.

"Surprise!" They all yelled together. It was only then that she understood the reason Applegate had insisted she meet him at the diner. This was her welcome home gathering!

Grinning, Brady looked down at her. "I was running a bit late out there."

"You could have warned me," Haley said out of the corner of her mouth, trying to quell her sudden sense of vulnerability.

"And ruined all their fun? My job is to keep the peace around here."

Chuckling, he watched as Haley was engulfed by a herd of old friends.

Sitting at the counter, Will watched the town welcome Haley. They'd done something similar when he'd moved back to town. There was nothing like the warmth of Mule Hollow. It was a place where once you belonged, you always belonged. But watching Haley's shell-shocked expression, he couldn't help wondering if the feeling was mutual.

Haley had created quite a life for herself in California, and by the almost robotic way she was receiving the hugs from everyone he was more than certain that she didn't share their feeling that she had "come home." Some things never changed.

She looked great, though. Will couldn't deny that the years had been good to Haley. Her skin glowed and her golden hair gleamed in the light like polished brass, setting off her green eyes. She had the most amazing eyes, big and expressive, they dominated her oval face. When she smiled though, when she really smiled, it was as if she lit up the world. At least that was how it had felt to him.

"Hey, buddy, you okay?"

Will glanced at Brady as he took the stool next to him at the counter. Turning away from watching Haley, Will picked up his coffee and nodded. "Yeah, I'm just suffering from aftershock."

"By the frown on your face I'd already figured that one out."

Will met Brady's sympathetic gaze. "That obvious?"

"'Fraid so."

"Brady, can you tell me why I came here this morning?"

"I could make an educated guess if you want me to."

Will shook his head. "Forget I asked. That's a can of worms I'd rather not open."

"I can tell you from experience that unfinished business has a way of catching up to you at one time or another."

Will drank his coffee instead of trying to come up with an answer. He could deny it all he wanted, but he'd come here this morning because every man had his weakness.

His happened to be Haley Bell Thornton.

Haley made it through the whirlwind of welcomes as she was led around the room by Applegate. His obvious joy at having her home was making her feel so ashamed. It had been six years since she'd been here for her grandmother's funeral.

She was a skunk, all right.

A selfish skunk.

Spotting Will sitting at the counter didn't help matters. It took every bit of her self-control not to turn around and run out of the diner. She didn't have the energy to face him this morning. This homecoming was hard enough on her guilt-ridden heart without having to face him, too. Especially in front of everyone.

"Will, here she is," Applegate called out

before she could figure a way around facing him again. She was appalled at Applegate's proclamation as he directed her toward Will.

"Haley," Will drawled, tipping his head toward her in greeting while his eyes bore into hers.

He wasn't wearing his hat and she couldn't help noticing that he still wore his thick sable hair in a traditional cut, parted on the left and combed back off his face. The cut accentuated the strength of his jaw and the prominence of his cheekbones. She was certain looking at him made women other than herself forget to breathe when looking at him. But enough of that.

She forced a smile and was certain it came out looking as if she'd swallowed a tablespoon of castor oil. "Will," she gritted out as Applegate looked expectantly from one to the other. His smile, so big that every tooth in his mouth showed, was the only reason Haley maintained her position.

She was shocked when suddenly Applegate slapped a hand on Will's shoulder, the sound cracking through the room like a backfire. "That ain't no way to say hello to the person what was almost yer intended. Give her a hug, son."

Stunned, Haley stared at her grandpa. *How could he?* Will had always been a gentleman, and Applegate was taking advantage of that fact. "That's okay," she gasped. "You don't have to get up."

A gleam she could only read as a challenge flashed through his dark gaze, and to her horror he stood up.

"App's right, Haley. The least I can do is give you a hug."

Before she could do anything to stop it, she found herself wrapped in Will's arms. *Oh my.* If she'd thought she was confused before—well she was a mess now. Because though it had been ten years since she'd left him at the altar, she had never forgotten how right it felt to be held in his embrace.

"See thar, ain't that nice," Applegate thundered.

As quick as it happened, it ended. Will suddenly dropped his arms and stepped back. Haley had been so stunned by the embrace that her arms remained limply at her sides. Where they belonged, she reminded herself.

His expression was unreadable and though she knew he'd hugged her to pacify her grandpa, the oddest sensation came over her when she looked into his stony eyes. *Had those eyes really once looked at her with love?* They were so distant now that it was tough to imagine such a thing.

"So how's your new ex-fiancé?"

His clipped words were spoken in a low voice, but those standing around watching them had no problem hearing them. Like a deflating balloon, Applegate's smile drooped into a heavy frown and a ripple of gasps could be heard behind her.

Startled, but not really surprised, she met Will's unflinching gaze with one of her own as she straightened her spine. If she'd learned one thing over the last few years, it was to stand her ground.

She lifted her chin. "I'm fairly certain that Lincoln is celebrating at this very moment. After all, he dodged a bullet."

Will lifted his eyebrow. "I can understand that perfectly. As I'm certain fiancé number two would, as well."

So he wanted to make a scene. *So much for him being a gentleman,* she thought, as her blood pressure inched upward. "Is that so?"

Not breaking eye contact with her, Will pulled money from his front pocket and slapped it onto the counter by his plate of uneaten eggs and bacon. "Believe me, darlin', the day you walked out on me was the best day of my life. I figure it saved me a costly divorce and a valley of trouble in between."

Haley's hands knotted into fists to keep them from shaking as darts of anger and humiliation shot through her. Other than the pounding of her heart that Haley hoped no one else could hear, the room had become as silent as a tomb. *Why had she come home?* It certainly hadn't been for this…this melodramatic confrontation.

With one last cold stare Will walked through the small crowd as it parted to make way for him. He never looked back as he hit the swinging door and disappeared into the cold morning light.

Which left Haley at the counter to face her friends alone.

As mad as she was at Will, she couldn't help thinking that it was about time she was the one being walked out on. She'd be the first to admit that she deserved it. At least in part. But that didn't mean she liked it, and it certainly didn't mean she was going to take that kind of treatment like the timid little mouse she'd once been.

"Ha!" she huffed in delayed reaction, then stormed out of the diner after him.

He was opening his truck door when she buzzed down the steps toward him. The loud shuffle of feet could be heard as the diners filed out onto the sidewalk behind her.

"Will Sutton," she snapped. "You can judge me and be angry at me if you want to because I left you standing at that altar ten years ago. But hey, guess what? I didn't see you coming to get me."

She'd almost gotten married three times, and the truth was that the only man of the three she'd expected or wanted to come after her had been Will. And he hadn't.

Why was that? He'd said he loved her. If you loved someone, didn't you try to hang on to them? Didn't you fight for them? Despite their argument and her bruised heart, she'd expected him to care enough to come after her. To try and make things right.

His cold stare raked over her. "It wouldn't have mattered if I came after you. You'd made your choice."

Speechless at his coldness, Haley watched him climb into his truck, back out onto Main Street then drive away. "It might have," she whispered into the chilling wind, knowing it was true. She'd been a young woman struggling with self-esteem and identity issues everyone around her seemed oblivious to. Especially the man who professed to love her. Despite what he thought, his coming after her would have mattered. That he didn't think so still stung. And, amazingly, proved he continued to have the ability to hurt her. Even after all these years.

Chapter Four

Haley bit her lip as she realized she'd just made a scene in front of everyone standing behind her. How could wounds so old feel so raw and fresh? She closed her eyes and struggled for calm. She and Will had planned to marry a week before Christmas ten years ago. Their almost wedding anniversary was coming up and, truth be told, there hadn't been a Christmas season that didn't pass without her thinking about what might have been…if only he'd cared enough.

Reeling in her emotions, Haley clasped her palms together and plastered on a smile as she watched him disappear down the street. She was determined that no one would know just how much she'd been shaken by Will Sutton's condemnation.

Condemnation.

Just who did the man think he was? She frowned, and her temper started escalating again. Sucking in a cleansing breath of cool air, she had to really concentrate to put on her saleswoman's face—the everything's-going-my-way face.

It was hard to do sometimes, but she wasn't making her way up the ladder of success by accident. Nope, she'd faced harder people than Will over the last few years, kept her wits about her and come out on top. She learned early on that many of her fellow real-estate agents would weasel and lie and connive to take her sales at every opportunity. Five- and six-figure commissions tended to bring out the worst in people. It had taken being tricked out of a few commissions and having to eat peanut butter for a month, but she'd finally smartened up and shucked the small-town gullibility…on the inside. On the outside she learned that her open and friendly face was her number-one moneymaker. Once she'd learned to watch her back and not trust anyone but herself, things had started to happen. Haley could smile with the best of them and charm her way right to the bank. The saying Don't Get

Mad, Get Even went a long way toward the truth.

Haley spun around, smile in place. "I don't know about all of you, but a good fight in the morning makes me so hungry I could eat a bear. How about it, Sam? It's been far too many years since I had your bacon and eggs."

To her surprise, everyone was smiling at her even before she'd turned around. It was a bit disconcerting, but instantly her fake smile turned genuine. She had forgotten just how sweet Mule Hollow residents could be.

"One plate of eggs and bacon coming up, Haley Bell," Sam said, holding the door for her as everyone parted and let her enter the diner first.

"See, what'd I tell y'all," she heard Applegate say to Norma Sue and Esther Mae as she passed by him. He was grinning, and Haley's heart felt good in that moment. Since her grandma Birdie had died, he just hadn't been the same. And though he didn't say much about it when they talked, Haley knew he missed her something fierce. Again, guilt settled on Haley's shoulders.

Before she could sink with the weight of it, the majority of people started telling her goodbye, streaming back out of the diner on their way to work. The exuberant salon owner, Lacy, whom Haley would easily have recognized from Molly Popp's description in the newspaper columns, threw her arms around her and hugged her. Then she dashed off. It was as if she were standing there one minute and—poof—she was gone with only the swinging door to prove that she had indeed been there. Haley was completely taken by surprise, and she couldn't help the chuckle that escaped her. So that was the woman who'd helped bring about this amazing change in Mule Hollow and its Main Street.

Haley decided then and there that she would make it a point to meet Lacy again.

"She's always like that," Esther Mae said. "We get a real kick out of that one."

"She seems really fun," Haley said and started to follow her grandpa back to his table.

"Oh, no you don't," Norma Sue said, grasping her by both shoulders and aiming her toward a booth. "Haley Bell, you come sit with us."

Haley glanced at Applegate and he started to protest, but Norma Sue cut him off. "Now remember, Applegate, you and Stanley have a checker game calling your names. Besides, you and Haley Bell can visit after y'all go home."

"That's right," Esther Mae said, pushing Haley into the booth then scooting in beside her so that Haley had to slide in fast or get sat on.

Immediately, Adela and Norma Sue sat down across the table and looked expectantly at her. Haley was surrounded, plain and simple. She couldn't have gotten away from their inquiring eyes if she wanted to.

"I just have to ask," Esther Mae cooed, leaning in and batting her lashes. "Who's your favorite movie star that you've met out there?"

"Well, I—" Haley started to answer but Esther Mae was so excited she kept right on going.

"I just love that Paul Newman. Cool Hand Luke. You know, that movie he was in, *Cool Hand Luke*. Oh, he just makes my heart pitter-patter thinking about it. Did you get to meet him yet?"

"Esther Mae," Norma Sue snapped. "Calm down, and let the girl talk. So did you? Did you meet Paul Newman? My favorite movie of his is *Hud*. You know, he was such a good bad boy. Just made you want to reform him yourself."

Esther Mae harrumphed. "Talk about hogging the conversation. How's she supposed to answer with you going on like that? So did ya?"

Haley met Adela's laughing blue eyes and smiled. "Yes. His main home is in Connecticut, but actually I did meet Mr. Newman and his lovely wife at a charity that I was attending just last month."

"No you didn't!" exclaimed Esther Mae. "You really did?"

Haley laughed and nodded. "I really did."

Norma Sue sighed and her eyes got all dreamy for a minute. "Was he as cute up close as he is in the movies?"

Haley assured them that he was.

"How about that Sean Connery?" Esther Mae asked.

Haley then gave the ladies a rundown of whom she'd met, who was nice and who she hoped to never have to see again. She was thankful when Sam ambled over with a pot of coffee and her plate of eggs and bacon. It smelled fabulous. Haley had tried becoming a vegetarian when she first left Mule Hollow, but her Texas roots went too deep. She loved bacon and steak, and though she usually ate chicken or fish, she planned to enjoy Sam's cooking to the fullest while she was here.

"So tell us about this last man you walked out on—"

"Esther Mae," Adela said in her soft voice. "Let's not pry into Haley's business."

Haley gave Adela a grateful smile, took a bite of crisp bacon and realized that at some point she would have to explain her actions. It was either get it out now or spend the rest of her visit dodging the subject.

"It's okay," she said, wiping her lips with her napkin.

"See," Esther Mae said, beaming. "I knew she'd tell us. We're practically family. Besides, all it takes is a good look at her to know she needs somebody to talk to. *And* that she's been working herself to the bone. Really, honey, you're so thin. You haven't had any of that liposuction, have you?"

Haley chuckled. She couldn't help it; the outspoken Esther Mae cracked her up. "No lipo for me," she said, stirring a packet of sugar into her coffee. Thin was fashionable where she lived. To fit in she had to stay "spit-shined and polished," as Applegate would have called it. "I work out regularly at the gym—I'm too chicken for anything else. Okay, here's the lowdown. His name is Lincoln Billings, and I shouldn't have agreed to marry him—"

"Not that I'm judging or anything," Sam said, coming over to top off her coffee and refill everyone else's. "But just 'cause a man asks ya to marry him don't mean ya gotta say yes."

"Sam," Norma Sue said, frowning and waving him off. "This here is woman talk, if you don't mind."

Sam bristled. "All I'm saying is Haley needs to learn to say no. Seems it'd save her on wedding dresses—"

"Sam, dear, it's okay." Adela placed her hand on his. "You have a very valid point. But we don't want to overwhelm Haley when she's only just come home. Especially after going through what she went through."

Sam looked down at his wife and melted before Haley's eyes. The man absolutely adored Adela.

"You're right." Beaming, he patted her hand then strutted toward the kitchen. For a tiny man, he suddenly looked nine feet tall.

"He is such a dear," Adela sighed, watching him go before meeting Haley's gaze. "You know, Haley, one day there's going to be a man who can truly win your heart and you won't want to run away anymore. I'll pray for you on that one."

Haley sobered, thinking that one already had won her heart. He'd also broken it. And though she'd tried to force her heart back together, she was starting to think it couldn't be done. She wondered if her hardened heart would ever truly let a man in again. She couldn't help thinking that it might be too late for her. Maybe that was why she'd said yes to Linc when she'd known better. He'd caught her on a low night, during a beautiful candlelit dinner, and for a little while she'd let herself be…different. She'd pretended that her heart wasn't jaded and cold.

But in the end it just hadn't been enough.

Three hours later, back at her grandpa's house, Haley put a call in to her office. It wasn't pretty.

"Haley, what is the matter with you?"

"Sugar, I'm tired. I told you that." Haley had just finished talking to Linc. It was just as she'd suspected—he was okay and already moving forward.

Unlike some people she knew, like her assistant, Sugar. There was silence over the telephone line, and she braced for more questions. Sugar didn't give up easily. That was one reason she made such a great assistant.

"Look, Haley, you are delusional if you think I'm buying that bit of nonsense. Something is up, and I know it. Look, I know you didn't love Lincoln, but, girl, I have never seen you pass up a good deal. And Lincoln Billings was a great deal. I don't mean to hurt your feelings, but I think you must be sick. I mean really sick. This isn't like you."

"Sugar, we've already been through this. It was exactly like me. I walked out on two other men before Linc. It's a pattern."

"True, but they weren't Lincoln Billings. With Linc you had it made."

"Sugar, stop it, you're not selling me a house. The only reason Linc wanted to marry me was because I was a challenge and he was bored. Once the challenge wore off he'd have grown bored again and I'd have joined the ranks of all his other exes."

"Well, hon, you're probably right about that…but, Haley, you would've had it made for a little while. I'm telling you, I'd have grabbed him up so fast—"

"Stop it, Sugar." Haley couldn't help smiling. Sugar was Sugar, her assistant by day but an aspiring actress on the side. If Haley thought *she* was in a cutthroat business, Sugar could really tell some horror stories. She'd bought into the whole Hollywood scene and was constantly auditioning for parts looking for her big break, knowing that every day that passed was another day taking her further away from her dream. But she was sweet and endearing, and Haley worried about her. Still, right now Haley just needed her to be her assistant and take instruction without all this chatter. "Sugar, I don't want to talk about Linc anymore. I talked to him before calling you and all is well. He's fine, I'm fine, so drop it."

"Oh, all right," she huffed into the line. "So if that's not what's got you so tied in knots, what is it? You just don't sound like yourself, Haley."

She didn't feel like herself, but she didn't tell her friend that. "Look, Sugar, I'm fine. Just keep your eyes and ears open, and if any spectacular opportunities arise that I need to know about call me. Cell phones are worthless here, but leave a message on the machine and I'll get back to you."

They said their goodbyes and, as soon as the line went dead, Haley felt isolated. Sugar was her connection to the world she'd come to know. The world she'd worked hard to belong to. So if that was true, then why was she back here in Mule Hollow? Why was she feeling so unsettled?

Haley covered her face with her hands then raked them through her hair as she stared out Applegate's kitchen window toward the barn. In a simpler time, she'd loved it here. Being homeschooled and living in a travel trailer was normal for many kids whose fathers worked the pipeline and whose mothers chose to travel with them. However, her parents chose to let her live with her grandparents because she'd loved it there so much when she was younger. But as a teen she'd grown restless and dreamed of more. Looking back, she realized that those dreams had overshadowed her love of the small-town life. Still she'd needed to leave. She knew that now. She'd had to prove herself by following her dreams. No matter what it had cost her.

Which was all the more reason for the turmoil she was feeling.

She might not be certain about why she'd come home, or why she'd felt the urgent need to come directly here after calling off her wedding, but she knew that she didn't regret having left Mule Hollow. She regretted only having hurt Will Sutton. And, she had to admit, the way he'd hurt her.

Not that it really mattered anymore, since they'd both moved on with their lives and it was obvious that he didn't want anything more to do with her.

Still he had hurt her badly. The pain had dulled over the years but it had taken time. Time to get past the questions that would sneak up on her when she least expected them. Questions such as why hadn't Will loved her enough to believe in her? To come after her? Sure, a person could ask, Why hadn't she loved him enough to stay? But things had been complicated. She'd only been in her junior year of high school when they started dating, while Will had been in his sophomore year of college. It still blew her away thinking about it.

They made plans together, plans to leave Mule Hollow, and then just before they were to marry he changed his mind. He decided that he didn't want to pursue a career in architecture. He wanted to throw all that away—

And he expected her to forgo any dreams she had, marry him anyway and be content. She loved him so much she almost did. But at the moment of truth, when she was about to enter the church, something inside clicked.

Didn't she have the right to stretch her wings? Was she always going to be everyone's little darling? The little "Haley Bell" no one took seriously? Or was she going to stand up for herself and reach for her dreams?

She decided she had every right to want more, and she fled.

What she hadn't ever been able to get over was that Will had let her.

Haley pushed aside thoughts of Will. She hadn't come home to think about him, of that she was certain. She heard Applegate's truck pull up outside. It was time for the two of them to have a serious talk about what the doctor had said about his health.

It dawned on her that maybe he was so distracted by his condition that this was the reason he'd failed to tell her Will had moved back to town. That was really a huge alarm for her because Applegate just didn't pass up things like that. Unless he wasn't himself.

And if he wasn't himself—Haley stopped her runaway thoughts as the back door opened and Applegate walked inside.

It was time for some answers.

Chapter Five

"Applegate, why have I let you talk me into this?" Haley sat in the truck beside her grandfather and stared at the bright blue building in front of her. As with all the buildings on Main Street now, each was painted a vibrant color and Mule Hollow's community center was periwinkle-blue with lemondrop trim. Inside the townspeople were holding the first call for the annual Christmas program. Instead of getting answers, she'd somehow let Applegate talk her into participating. The man had a way of looking so pitiful that she couldn't say no. Especially since she was going to be here and she wanted to spend time with him, and since he was going to be at practice most evenings, it only made sense that she help him out.

After all, he clearly wasn't feeling too well, and since he'd refused to fess up to what was wrong with him, it was all the more reason for her to stay close by his side. Case in point, here she was about to get out and follow him into the building. A packed building judging by the number of cars and trucks sitting along the sidewalks.

"Well, are ya comin'?" Applegate asked, standing at the door looking back at her.

With an odd sense of foreboding she got out of the truck and trudged up the steps. She'd changed into a flowing skirt of turquoise-and-gold paired with a shimmering blouse—a sleeveless blouse because that was all she had with her and she hadn't made it to the store as planned. Needless to say she was cold. She had bare arms and strappy sandals! On top of her summer attire, she wore her grandmother's red wool short coat. It made a fashion statement like none Haley had seen since the day in kindergarten when she'd insisted on wearing her pink tutu to school with her brown riding boots. That had been a Haley Bell moment she'd heard about until the day she'd left town.

Haley stood for a moment in the chill, tugging the collar up as she lifted her chin and straightened her shoulders. She might be reduced to looking like that poor little klutz of a girl she used to be, but all she had to do was remember that she wasn't little *Haley Bell*. She was Haley Thornton. Confident career woman, rising star, a force to be reckoned with.

And clothes did not make the woman, the woman made the clothes.

Never let them see you sweat. *That's right.*

Chin up, smile on, she stepped onto the sidewalk determined to make the most of this night.

Standing on the planks, she smiled. She'd thought many times as she'd walked down the paved sidewalks of Rodeo Drive about Mule Hollow's plank sidewalks. They were so "Dodge City" and so far removed from the life she had now.

Looking up, she found her grandpa staring at her, his normal hound-dog scowl softened around the eyes. Automatically her heart puddled; she did love him so. "What?" she asked softly, stopping beside him.

"You look like yer grandmother standing there in that purdy little red coat. My how she did love that coat. I kin remember the day she bought it up in Ranger at the discount store.

You know yer grandmother, nothing fancy fer her, but she said red was a girl's best friend and it just put a spring in her step every time she tugged it on."

Haley's eyes misted at the remembrance that was so Grandma Birdie. A no-nonsense dynamo, Birdie Thornton had been a woman to admire. Applegate had always said Haley had her genes, yet until she'd moved away, Haley had never really thought so. She couldn't imagine Birdie ever having doubts about anything.

Haley leaned in and kissed Applegate's cheek. "Thank you for that reminder." He winked at her and held the door open. Haley ran a hand lovingly down the red coat and stepped inside the crowded room, no longer thinking about how the little coat clashed with her outfit, but how glad she was to feel her grandmother's embrace.

Just as she'd thought, the conference room was full. That didn't keep Lacy and Norma Sue from immediately spotting her and whisking Haley into the crowd, introducing her to anyone she hadn't met at the diner that morning. Haley was amazed at how the town had grown. There were couples—of all ages—everywhere. And they looked so happy. As everyone took their seats, she found herself studying them. These couples had something she'd known was missing with each of the men she'd left at the altar. The closest she'd come to finding happiness like that was with Will, but she'd been wrong. Looking at the couples around her now, Haley promised herself that the next time she was tempted to say yes to a wedding proposal, if there was a next time, she wouldn't say it unless she knew it was right. She wanted to feel something inside that would say, "This is the one."

The door opened at that moment and Will stepped inside. Haley's pulse jumped as if she were a track star who'd just heard the starting gun go off. It wasn't fair that the man had only gotten better looking with age. It was as if he were Clint Black or something, ageless. Not wanting him to catch her staring, she forced her gaze to Lacy, who was standing behind the podium holding a stack of papers.

Despite shifting her gaze, Haley remained aware of Will as he moved toward the back of the room. She wished she had a pair of blinders on to cut her peripheral vision to nothing. Maybe then she could concentrate on what Lacy was saying. As it was, she could see Lacy just chatting away, but Haley wasn't hearing a word she was saying. Oh, no. Haley was unwillingly tuned in to Will's quiet hellos to everyone he passed. Determined to ignore him, Haley gave Lacy her full attention.

"—casting's done on the play," she was saying. "But today we're getting the behind-the-scenes committees set up. We are going to have so much fun with this Christmas program!"

Lacy's enthusiasm was contagious. The play was going to be a look at what it might have been like for Mary and Joseph when they returned to his hometown after Joseph took Mary to be his wife. Audiences would be able to feel what they may have gone through because they were doing what God asked of them. Earlier when Applegate talked her into helping, he'd told her all about it and it sounded intriguing.

Fortunately for Haley, there was no acting involved for her. She'd agreed to come only to help with the props, a job she'd enjoyed during high school. She was pretty artistic, although when it came to swinging a hammer she was all thumbs and there were plenty of Haley Bell stories to prove it. Now Will, he was good with a hammer.

She found herself glancing toward the back of the room, where he stood, legs planted shoulder width apart, arms crossed as he focused on what Lacy was saying. Her pulse jumped again just looking at him and she quickly focused forward once more. She certainly hoped he wasn't on her team. The thought of having to work close to him just didn't settle well. There was so much past between them that it was obvious they would only bring turmoil to the present effort. And that wouldn't be good for anyone.

Lacy started reading off the list of committees. There was the costume committee—something Haley would never be on, seeing as how the one time she'd tried to hem a dress she'd accidentally sewn the skirt of the dress she was wearing to the dress her grandmother was teaching her to hem. Then there was the food committee, the marketing committee, makeup committee and onward down the line until last, but not least, the props committee. A sense of dread started filling Haley with each committee list that was called out and Will's name didn't appear. When Lacy started reading the props committee members, Haley knew she was doomed even before their names were read back-to-back. It was everything she could do to keep the alarm she felt from showing in her expression as she felt gazes bouncing off her at every angle. She swallowed hard and though her palms were perspiring she kept her hands still, not allowing herself to wipe them on her skirt for fear everyone would see that she was sweating. It was a trait she'd learned when negotiating property contracts. But this was different. This was more personal. She didn't want to be stuck on a team with Will. The man was a spur in her past that she didn't want to revisit. If she'd known he was living back in Mule Hollow she probably wouldn't have come home. There was no way she wanted to spend time with him.

But it was done. There was nothing she could do about it and not look suspicious. Not to mention how it would disappoint her grandpa.

She forced herself to think positively. She was a big girl now. This was a good time to wipe the slate clean. She could pull Will Sutton's ever-present memory from out of the dark closet she'd stuffed it in all those years ago and expose it to the light—then move on with her life. Her California dream life. A life that was wonderful, and fulfilling, and…and everything she'd ever wanted.

She straightened in her chair.

This was a good thing.

A step forward. That was what this experience would be. A big gigantic step toward…her future.

Chapter Six

Will didn't miss the look that passed between Norma Sue and Esther Mae the minute the names were read. The moment he heard Lacy call out Haley's name, he zeroed in on the two known matchmakers. He hadn't even realized Haley was going to help with the program. Now he was pretty sure he was being set up. But why? Why would anyone want to do that?

He thought Haley would be gone by the weekend, and now he realized that she must be staying. He needed a cup of coffee to digest that bit of information. He strode toward the table where cookies and a coffee-pot sat. Listening to Lacy continue to describe all that needed to be done before the big production in five weeks, his brain rolled over the time he didn't have that was going to be required of him for this. It was going to be a tight squeeze to get it all done, but it was the thought of spending time with Haley that filled him with dread.

He should have seen it coming. Haley could draw anything, so it was logical that Applegate had recruited her. Trying to shake the unease rising in him, Will took a cautious swallow of hot coffee and studied her profile. She looked as tense as he felt, no doubt just as wary as he was of this development. There was no denying that she would be a big help to the program. And the program was what this was all about. He should just relax and ignore the red flags he was seeing—

"Somethin' on yer mind?"

Applegate suddenly slapped him on the shoulder in greeting. Will sloshed coffee down the front of his jeans and glanced at the older man. He hadn't realized anyone was in the kitchen behind him, especially Applegate. He had no idea how long App had been watching Will stare at his granddaughter.

"No sir," he said, taking a quick swig of the scalding liquid and feeling the inside of his mouth fire up as he met Applegate's gaze. Will made a concerted effort to keep his eyes off Haley when they automatically started to slide back in her direction. He couldn't afford to let himself slip up like that again. The last thing he needed was to start speculation that he was standing in the back of the building staring longingly at Haley…. It might have been true, but that didn't mean he wanted everyone to notice he still had feelings for her.

To his dismay, instead of heading back to his chair, Applegate planted himself beside Will, folded his thin arms across his chest and settled in. He was so thin he reminded Will of a praying mantis as he cut his eyes toward Will and caught him staring.

"I figure we're gonna be puttin' in some long hours ta get this stage setup designed and finished in time," he said, raising a bushy brow.

Will relaxed a bit, relieved that Applegate wanted to talk about the program. "You're right about that. But I didn't see anything in those plans that requires welding. Why do they need me?" he asked.

Applegate cleared his throat loudly and shifted from foot to foot. His dour expression remained, but Will read his body language. Applegate was hedging. "We hoped you could come up with some easier way to help move the sets around." He cut his gaze at Will. "Ken ya do that? Plus, I got you on the drawing team. It ain't jest your welding that gotcha on my crew."

Dread settled over Will at the mention of drawing. He had a feeling he and Haley were going to be spending a lot of time together. Looking away, he focused on Lacy as she waved her hands to get everyone's attention again.

"Time to break up into individual groups so team leaders can set up work schedules," she called out, her face beaming. "All cast members see me."

Will hadn't known Lacy long, but it was obvious she had a heart for Mule Hollow. He'd moved home to help keep the town alive, but it was evident that Lacy had come here, set the town on her shoulders and was pushing with all her might to make it a place people wanted to set roots in. He liked her, and watching her get this production together he could fully understand how she'd been able to talk a bunch of dusty cowboys into painting their town the colors of a Joseph's coat of many colors. He smiled as she waved her arms over her head then met her husband Clint's gaze and sent him a kiss airmail. Something tugged inside Will watching the affection that passed between his old friend and his new wife. Will had always wanted that, but he'd resigned himself to the fact that he would probably never have it.

A flash of red caught his eye and, as quick as that, he was watching Haley again as she removed the little red coat she'd been wearing. The room was warm as toast, but when she slipped her graceful arms from the wool coat, he wished the heat would stop working. It was obvious that she'd stayed in shape, though she did look a bit thin to him. She probably worked out alongside the rich and famous at one of those preppy little gyms. After all, networking was a fact of life in any business, especially Haley's profession. If you wanted to be successful, you had to go where your clients were—and looking at the tanned, lean muscles of Haley's arms and her trim figure clad in the shimmering sleeveless top and flowing skirt that clung to her hips then flared out about her legs in a soft swirl of vibrant cloth, it was more than apparent that she must know all about networking.

"Hey, Will, what's up?" Sheri Gentry said, sailing past him to grab the coffeepot. Will sidestepped out of the way. Everyone knew that Sheri, the local nail tech and co-owner with Lacy of the salon Heavenly Inspirations, was a coffee-drinking dynamo. She and her husband, Pace, had just arrived back from a trip to Australia and like Haley, Sheri had a tan that wouldn't quit.

"Not much, Sheri. How's life treating you?"

She glanced at him over her shoulder. "Peachy."

Will chuckled then found himself glancing back toward Haley. He was so surprised to find her walking his way that he almost dropped his cup. He'd been out of line at their last meeting. If they were going to be working together, he had to be a man about it and act like an adult. That meant holding his tongue and keeping the past in the past.

Haley stopped beside Applegate, resting a hand on App's crossed arms and lifting an eyebrow. "Interesting group we have for the prop production."

It wasn't a question but a forthright statement that said she, too, hadn't missed that they were on the same team. And she had her suspicions. Applegate's expression didn't change at all. He looked from Haley to Will. "We needed persons with creativity and abilities, and the two of you fit the bill purdy perfect. I 'spect the good Lord was smiling on us when He brought the two of you back here. So, of course, I picked the both of you fer the design team. Now, I got me a good group of painters and such, but seein' how the two of you is so good at drawin' I figured y'all kin git in here first, draw up the different sets Lacy's askin' fer and then we kin pull the others away from their other projects to paint."

Will met Haley's gaze and couldn't miss her look of displeasure. Well, he wasn't any more thrilled at being thrown in with her than she was. All the years since she'd abandoned him at the altar had left him with emotions he tried to keep buried deep. There was no way of getting around the fact that he'd thought all these years that he still loved her. But he'd realized just this week that there was indeed a fine line between love and hate. And though he didn't hate Haley, these feelings he'd been carrying around couldn't still be love. More likely they were a mixture of hurt, loss and longing for what she'd left behind.

Those feelings seemed to be bubbling to the surface as raw today as they'd been the day he'd met her gaze across the church full of wedding guests and seen her shut down on him. He'd known in that instant that he'd lost her. When she'd turned and run from the church, he hadn't moved. He'd locked up, knowing she'd made her choice.

Back in those days Haley had had the most expressive eyes Will had ever seen. They'd had their first fight over his decision not to leave Mule Hollow only days prior to the wedding, and he'd read in the flare of her gaze that she'd chosen to follow her heart. And her heart hadn't included him. If it had, she'd have respected his decision to seek a simpler life in the town he loved. She'd have chosen to marry him, raise a family and build a quiet life in a place with values—the place he'd felt in his heart was the right place to be. Haley had made it clear that their vision of life was not the same, so he'd let her go.

Yet all these years he'd thought he still loved her. He must have been wrong. He didn't even know her.

How could you love someone you don't even know?

* * *

There he went, looking at her as if she were gum stuck to the bottom of his shoe. Haley had a bad feeling about this entire setup, and with the way Will was looking at her, it was easy to see he thought this was all her idea. Well, if he thought she was any more pleased at this turn of events than he was, he had another think coming. The last place she wanted to be was spending the time with him that it was evident this project was going to require. This had not been in her plans for returning to Mule Hollow.

There was no way she and Will were the only semi-artistic people in this entire room. Applegate had something up his scrawny little sleeve. The fact that he suddenly wouldn't look at her was a big clue. But why? That was the question. What could he possibly gain by throwing her into a situation that required her to work so closely with Will?

"So," she said. "It seems we are on the same team." Like she'd acknowledged earlier, she was taking steps forward and if that meant spending time around Will then so be it. Meanwhile, she needed to keep her cool around Will so that no one would get any silly ideas that she was nervous or fluttery around him. Fluttery, an odd word, but it fit because her insides were feeling like the wings of a thousand butterflies. Maybe Will Sutton made her nauseated.

"And you two are going to have yor work cut out fer ya. That's why I picked ya. Haley, we were picking teams the day you drove into town—like I told y'all, if that ain't a God thang then I don't know what is. Instantly, I remembered that time back when you was in high school and y'all built that puppet set for the elementary school. You remember that?"

Staring up at Will, Haley couldn't help remembering how much fun they'd had coming up with the design and building it together. Will had been home from college, and she'd come up with the idea and he'd jumped right in to help her. "We did have fun," she confessed, knowing there was no way to deny it. The admission startled Will. It showed in his eyes and the way he shifted his head to the side as he studied her. Haley liked that she'd surprised him. He needed to realize she was capable of moving on.

"Didn't we?" she asked him, lifting an eyebrow when it suddenly occurred to her the feeling could have been one-sided.

He nodded first, then answered, "Yes, we did."

Applegate snorted. "Yup, this'll work. I kin tell these thangs."

Haley wasn't so sure about it, but she couldn't help smiling at the satisfaction radiating from her granddad.

It was nice to see she was at least making him happy—even if it left her feeling, well, fluttery.

Chapter Seven

The following day, with a mixture of dread and an undeniable nagging sense of curiosity, Haley pulled up the drive to Will's house. She kept reminding herself that she was making her grandpa happy and doing Mule Hollow a service while she was in town relaxing. *Relaxing, ha!*

She hadn't known just how much she'd needed a break until now. Her life had become a whirlwind of meetings and showings, a race to secure the right clients and sell the right properties. After only a few days in Mule Hollow, with its slow pace and country charm, she was startled to see just how much she'd needed to slow down. At least for a few weeks. And she was relaxing…when she didn't think about Will.

She could help with the props for the production even if she wouldn't be around for opening night. Already, her bosses were pushing to know when she was coming back. She'd hedged, but she didn't know how long that could go on.

She pushed that aside, though. Today, she was here to discuss sketches. Leave it to Applegate to suggest she and Will work alone the first week designing the sets. When they were ready they could call the rest of the team in for the actual building and painting. Haley wanted to protest, but she kept her mouth shut. Will hadn't protested or made any kind of complaint, so she certainly wasn't going to say anything. She didn't want it to look as if she had any reason for not wanting to work alone with him. So here she was at his house.

About to be alone with him.

She wouldn't focus on that. Instead, she studied his house and tried to settle down. White sandstone with cedar posts and a green metal roof. It was the same home he'd grown up in, but she could see that it had been updated. The metal roof replaced the more traditional shingles, and the room that was lined with floor-to-ceiling windows along the right side of the house was also a new addition. She studied it as she followed the drive around the house. When they'd made plans to meet today, Will had told her to pull her car around back to the shop. The concrete drive spread out into a large round circle at the back of the house. The "shop" turned out to be a smaller version of the house. It sat on the far side of the drive facing the back of the house. Its two garage doors stood open despite the cold.

After parking her car, Haley climbed out then walked toward the sounds coming from the shop. She found Will standing with his back to her as he worked, Alan Jackson's song "Remember When" blasting from the radio speakers next to the door. Haley stood still, startled by the sight of Will and the poignant song. She could do nothing but watch Will for a moment.

He wore boots, scuffed and worn, just like a cowboy liked them. His jeans were pale blue with a white crease line running up the back that marked many washes and stiff starches. She knew the same mark would run parallel up the front of the jeans, accenting the lean length of his legs. Legs that were still, after all these years, so perfectly proportioned with his trim waist and wide shoulders. In his hand he held a torch, and Haley watched as he used it to cut along the sketch on the huge sheet of steel. It was immediately apparent that he was far from a novice at using the flame like a scalpel. She was instantly fascinated watching him work his craft.

It took her a moment to realize her heart was doing a drum solo inside her chest, completely at odds with the slow hypnotic voice of Alan Jackson imploring her to "remember when." She readily complied, her memory tumbling back—easily remembering Will's laugh as they raced along the dry riverbed during the first thunderstorm of the summer. The first feel of his arms as they came around her. The first kiss they'd shared…oh, she remembered all right.

As if sensing he wasn't alone, he turned around. Slowly, he lifted the protective glasses he wore and met her gaze with steady eyes.

"Haley."

Haley snapped to, managing a tight smile. "I didn't mean to startle you," she said, her heart thundering.

He shut down the torch and laid it on the steel beside the protective glasses. His hair was flat against his forehead, giving him a youthful appearance—just as she remembered…

Haley pushed the memories away and walked over to look at his work, hoping her expression didn't show that she'd just taken a long slow walk down memory lane.

Looking at his art gave her the cover she needed. She was astounded by it. He'd always been creative and artistic, and she'd admired his own entrance gate when she'd turned onto his drive. Like the piece she was looking at now, she'd been blown away by the intricacy of it.

"This is phenomenal," she said, looking at the cutout of a cowboy riding a bucking bronc.

He turned to stand beside her. "Thank you."

She couldn't help reaching out to touch it, to trace the outline with her finger. "It's round," she said, stating the obvious. "What will you do with it?"

"I'll make a steel band that it will set in, and then I'll mount it in that. Like a cameo."

He gestured toward a rectangular gate frame filled with bars except for the center. It was going to be a massive gate. A piece of art itself.

To her relief, Will moved away from her. "I'll set it today, then powder coat it black and mail it out next week."

Haley followed him with her gaze then studied the rest of the room. There were many of the rectangular frames already built in various sizes around the room. Though they were empty, she couldn't help wondering what would end up in them.

Applegate had told her that Will was very busy. She could see why. Her gaze boomeranged back around and met his.

"Did you bring the play and Lacy's wish list of scenes?"

Unnerved by his closeness, Haley put on her game face and waved the notebook. "Where do you want to discuss it?"

He continued to study her for another minute, his expression blank. "Come up to the house. It's warmer there. I tend to work with the doors open."

She wanted to say no. That they should just get to work and get this over with. Instead, glad to leave the awkward moment behind them, she followed him in silence up the walk, past the flower beds that were brimming with pansies, their little purple and yellow faces calmly holding their own in the cold morning air. Will had always had a way with plants, a trait he'd inherited from his father. It was a quirk she'd liked about him. Not many young men actually enjoyed fiddling with flowers. Will hadn't ever seemed to mind that the other cowboys teased him about it.

Looking at his handiwork, Haley took heart from the strength of the dainty flowers facing the chill. "So," she said, turning to the safety of small talk. "I love what you've done with the place. Where are your parents now?"

"They moved to Austin a few years back. They wanted to be closer to my sister and her kids, and Dad wanted to get my mom closer to her doctors. She's had some health issues."

"I'm sorry to hear that." And she was. His parents were lovely people. His mother was an especially gracious and godly woman. "I'm sure being near Terri and the kids is good for her."

"We think so."

He held the door for her, and she brushed past him as she stepped into the kitchen of his home. It was an odd feeling to step into the house she'd thought she would share.... Haley pushed the thought away.

She was a strange, strange woman. A week ago she'd been about to marry another man, and here she was now reminiscing about Will Sutton.

"Can I take your coat?"

She jumped at the sound of his voice so close beside her and at the touch of his hands on her shoulders. He was only touching her to help her out of her coat, for goodness sake.

"Oh, sure. Thank you. It's warm here…I freeze—"

"I remember."

She met his gaze over her shoulder and a ridiculous little tremor raced along her spine. He remembered.

"Yes, well," she laughed, her nerves showing. "I'm sure you would. I complained enough."

Yanking her arms free of the coat, she all but ran away from him, totally mad at her weak knees. But he smelled so good. Always had.

Lifting her chin, she walked to the far side of his kitchen, putting as much space between them as possible. She leaned her hip against the counter, wrapped her arms across her waist and watched him hang her coat on the rack next to the door. The room rang with the silence.

There was nothing between them. *Nothing.*

Hadn't been for almost a decade, yet she was at a loss for words. She'd better get over it or this project wasn't ever going to get finished. Besides, he wasn't showing any emotion at all.

"Can I offer you something to drink? Coffee, soda?"

She shook her head. "No thanks," she said, intent on getting to work. "How did you start doing gates?" That was not what she'd intended to ask. She'd intended to tell him it was time to get to work. She didn't need to know any personal details about his life.

He opened the refrigerator and turned his back to her as he studied the interior. "After you left, I went ahead and used my degree in architecture, but I wasn't happy with my work. So, when I discovered a way out I never looked back."

"I see." Haley nodded, thinking she heard a double meaning to the words *never looked back*. She decided now was a perfect time to put them back on track...before she said something she might regret. "I think the drawings will be fairly easy to sketch out," she said, feeling stiff and awkward.

He turned, holding a pitcher of tea. The man had always loved sweet tea. It was amazing with all that sugar that he'd kept such a sleek physique—that she had no business admiring. What a dope she was!

She swung around, flopped open the notebook she'd laid on the counter and studied the first idea. She concentrated hard on it. They were going to open the story up with Mary and Joseph arriving home after becoming man and wife. They needed a backdrop of the interior of their home. There was also a small bridge in several scenes. "Have you thought any about the bridge?" she asked, listening to him fill glasses with ice and feeling as if she was coming down with a case of the shakes.

"Actually, I already started it. I couldn't sleep after the meeting last night so I went out to the shop, and the next thing I knew I was building a bridge."

She smiled at him over her shoulder, despite her growing discomfort. "You never were much of a procrastinator." He didn't smile, but the corner of his lips curved slightly. A frog suddenly settled in Haley's windpipe, and she was grateful for the tea he handed her. Their fingers brushed as she took the glass, and Haley felt the touch all the way to her toes. Will pulled his hand away, seemingly unaffected.

She was obviously crazy.

"I don't have a lot of time to waste," he said, sipping his tea.

The clock above the stove ticked the seconds out as they stared at each other. "Then we're in the same boat. I have a job to get back to. So the sooner we get it done, the quicker both of us can get on with our lives." There, she felt better. She met his steady gaze straight on.

Tick. Tick. Tick.

"Right," he agreed.

Haley watched his Adam's apple bob.

Tick. Tick. Tick.

"Sooo, let's get to it," she said, swinging back toward the papers on the counter.

When Will stepped up beside her, leaning over the papers to study them, her heart jumped—again. What was she doing? This was crazy. She couldn't take it— "Okay," she snapped, pushing away from the counter and the inch that separated their arms from touching. She stomped across the room to the far counter and swung around to glare at him. "I can't do this." *No, Haley, no!*

He turned to stare at her. All it took was the blank expression on his face to send her blood pressure through the roof! "That does it! Stop with the blank looks. You're the one who blew up at me the other day and now every time I'm around you look like a wax dummy in a museum. We are walking on eggshells, and I can't stand it."

He lifted a perfect thick eyebrow. Other than that, his expression didn't change.

"Say something. You had plenty to say when we had an audience."

His brows creased, and his lips flattened. "All that was just reaction from the shock of seeing you after all these years. That's all it was. We have been put on a project together, and all I want is to get through it like two adults and move on. I realized that there really is no sense in rehashing our sordid past."

"Sordid. Meaning my walking out on you."

"Call it whatever you want. I don't really care."

"I get that clearly. I got that clearly all those years ago and that's why I left. You never really did get it."

The room grew silent again all but for the

ticking of the clock and the sound of Haley's heart pounding in her chest.

"Look, I really can't do this." She headed toward the back door. There was no use fighting this. He was bent on trying to make her feel bad and she wasn't going to give in to that. She refused to just pretend it wasn't happening. He knew and she knew that he could take care of the drawing of the props without her, so there was no sense in her having to stress out over being around him.

She yanked her coat off the rack, threw open the door and stormed onto the porch.

"What do you want from me?"

His words stopped her halfway down the steps. She swung toward him, fighting an embarrassing need to cry. Cry! She didn't cry. "I want you to admit you were partly to blame for what happened between us."

By the look in his eyes, she knew he still didn't get it and that he never would. To him, he hadn't done anything wrong. It was all her fault.

She shook her head and shrugged her shoulders. "And that right there assures me that I made the right decision."

Spinning away, she stalked down the brick

path and got into her car. She didn't even look back to see if he was still standing on the porch.

His fault! Who was she kidding? Haley had turned her back on everything they'd had between them, and she wanted to blame it on *him?*

Well, he may have been a fool in love all those years ago, but he wasn't one any longer. He'd been pining away for her all this time—and for what? A woman who saw nothing except herself. That wasn't the kind of woman he wanted to love.

Will closed his eyes and let the cold air seep into him. Hardening his resolve, he refused to listen to the small voice that was trying to get his attention. He went back into the kitchen, snatched up the props sketchbook and stormed into his office.

He didn't need Haley Bell Thornton to do this job. He'd didn't need Haley Bell Thornton, period.

Chapter Eight

"Haley, what are you doin' here?"

Haley slammed the door of her car and stalked toward Applegate. He was sitting on his front porch peeling a green apple. "We need to talk, Granddad."

"Well, I kin tell ya got a spur in yor saddle so sit down and talk."

Haley settled into the chair beside him and brought her knees up so she could wrap her arms around them, partly to block out the cold air and partly to comfort her frazzled nerves. "Whatever you have planned for me and Will isn't going to work."

Applegate kept peeling the apple. "I ain't got any idea what yer talking about."

"I don't believe you," she said, staring at him with hooded eyes.

He met her accusing gaze straight on. "Well that's a fine thing to say to yer poor ol' grandpa."

Haley tightened her arms around her knees and rested her chin on top, fortifying herself with the hug. "There's nothing poor about you. You're as smart as a whip and as cunning as they come. And don't think I don't know it."

His eyes shifted briefly, then held hers. "Haley Bell, you spend yer life running from weddings. You ever thank it was Will you shouldn't have run away from?"

"Applegate," she warned. "There's more to the story than you know."

"And if you don't tell me what it is then I won't know what that is, now will I?"

Haley hesitated to share her personal life with anyone. Even her granddad. "Look, you're just going to have to believe me. Will Sutton was never the right man for me. I'll find the right one some day. Until then, don't get your hopes up. And don't think I haven't picked up on the fact that you and the ladies are having romantic ideas about the two of us. That's nonsense."

Applegate sliced a piece of apple and took the whole piece into his mouth, chewing slowly. She was not fooled. He was thinking of the right response. But she wasn't waiting around. "You have been evading the issue of your health for the past two days. Tell me exactly what the doctor said about the problems you've been having. Tell me, please. I don't like being in the dark. I'm worried sick."

"Well," he sighed and shook his head. "I didn't want ta tell ya, but I've got the Zackly disease."

Haley slid her feet to the ground as alarm shot through her. "Zackly disease? What is it? Can it be cured? Are you in pain?" All kinds of questions bombarded her as she racked her brain for anything she'd ever heard about the disease.

Applegate suddenly looked pensive. "Now, don't go gettin' all riled up. I told ya it ain't nothin' to worry about."

"Granddad, I worry, okay? Tell me what's wrong with you."

He dropped his gaze to the floor and mumbled. Haley's ears perked up.

"*What* did you say?" Haley asked, catching a few of his mumbled words. Enough to know she was about to be madder than a hornet.

"I said, I don't *zackly* have nothin' wrong."

"Applegate Thornton!" She shot out of her chair. "How could you do that? This is not funny. It's not. Stop that chuckling."

He chuckled harder, his drooping face coming alive with laughter. She slammed down into her chair and, despite her anger at him, found herself smiling. He always had been a prankster. Her grandmother always said there were times in their marriage he'd almost driven her crazy with his jokes. Especially the times he'd told her something and then forgot to right it. Like the time he said that the singer Phil Collins was the same guy who played the character Ernest T. Bass and threw rocks at everyone on *The Andy Griffith Show.* Her grandma Birdie hadn't believed him for the longest time, then he'd finally convinced her he was telling the truth. She'd promptly told all of her friends and, despite most of them telling her she was wrong, she'd argued the fact. Applegate sure had hated to face the music when he'd realized a week later he'd neglected to tell her it was a joke.

"Has all this just been a big joke?" Haley asked now, knowing the truth before she asked the question.

At least he had the decency to look slightly

ashamed. "Haley Bell. Come on, now. The doctor told me he thought I had an ulcer, but he didn't know fer sure. He had to do some test to know *exactly*. I didn't thank it was nuttin' to be gettin' all riled up about. Certainly didn't figure ta tell ya about it on the phone, but then you broke the news that you was thinking about gettin' married again— and well, I gotta bad feeling and needed a reason to try and git you home. I been wanting to see you ferever anyway." His face drooped back into a frown once more. "It ain't right that a poor old grandpa has ta fib about being sick to git his granddaughter to come see him."

Shame melted Haley's heart. "You're right, Grandpa." She hopped from the chair and hugged him tight. "I am so sorry. I've been so busy trying to prove myself…I just forgot what was important is all."

She kissed his cheek then sat back in her chair. "I promise when I go back to Beverly Hills, I'll make it a point to come back more often. But you've got to stop telling me fibs about your health."

He harrumphed, surprising her with his stern gaze.

"Haley, you don't belong out thar. You

belong here. Kin't you see that Mule Hollow needs a real-estate agent? Why, we're gettin' more and more folks wantin' to move out here. That agent out of Ranger's tryin', but that's seventy miles away and she's got her hands full in her own town."

For the briefest moment, Haley wondered what it would be like selling property in a rural setting. No glitz and glamour. She pushed the thought aside. She was good at what she did. She'd worked hard to get where she was. Not to mention, well, she didn't think she could live in the same town with Will. There was simply too much of a strain when she was around him. And she felt completely out of her element when she was near him. The morning fiasco proved it. Every time they were near each other, she acted irrationally. Storming out of his house like a teenager. How could she have done that? It was embarrassingly adolescent.

If she was honest with herself, Will and everyone who knew her were probably having a hard time keeping their faces straight when they were around her.

After all these years of striving to be taken seriously, of trying to be more than little

Haley Bell with her oddball mishaps, she'd accomplished nothing, really.

Absolutely nothing.

It was almost laughable even to her.

It was just so absolutely *Haley Bell* of her!

The thought was depressing. "Don't get your hopes up. I could never live here again, Grandpa."

"Haley Bell, a girl like you can do anything ya want to do. That's what I don't git about all this."

That was exactly what she was trying to say. No one understood her, never had and it seemed never would.

Will realized right after he watched Haley drive away that he was going to have to figure out a way to put his feelings aside and be able to look at Haley without getting knots in his stomach. They were not kids, after all, and she'd been perfectly right.... They were walking on eggshells when they were around each other. It needed to stop. He needed to dig deep, work with her while she was home, and watch her leave again.

Then his life would return to normal. He'd carved out a decent life for himself. He didn't need Haley.

So he gave himself and Haley an hour to calm down, then he went after her. It was the right thing to do.

He found Applegate sitting on his front porch.

"'Bout time you showed up," he called the second Will closed the door of his truck. "You had my Haley Bell madder than a swarm a hornets."

Will shifted from one boot to the other, uncomfortable that Applegate knew they'd argued. "I apologize about that, sir."

"No need for apologies to me. A good fight now and agin keeps the blood flowing."

Will didn't want to point out that his blood had been flowing fine before Haley showed up. "Is Haley around?" he asked, watching as Applegate whittled the head of what looked like a small duck. It was cool but the older man didn't seem the least bit worried about the chill in the air. The sun was out and with a light jacket on it was pleasant.

"Nope," Applegate said, spitting a sunflower seed into a bucket at his feet. The sound made a small ping as it hit dead center. App and his buddy Stanley were sunflower-seed maniacs. They bought them by the five-pound bags down at Pete's Feed & Seed store and steadily chewed them as they played checkers down at the diner. They'd tried getting away with spitting the shells on the floor at one time, but Sam had put a stop to that right quick. Of course, the two checker players argued that there were restaurants in Ranger that supplied the peanuts and *told* patrons to throw the shells on the floor when they were done. Sam had been quick to point out that there was a big difference in throwing shells on the floor and spitting shells on the floor.

Will glanced toward Haley's high-powered sports car parked in the drive. "Can you tell me where I can find her?" The thought of her driving a car like that was a little scary to Will. But he reminded himself that she wasn't his to worry about, and she could drive what she wanted.

"Maybe," Applegate said, gazing up from beneath his fuzzy caterpillar eyebrows. "Don't need ya going out thar givin' her a hard time, though. She didn't come all the way out here from California to be harassed by the likes of an old flame."

Will stepped back. Is that what she'd told him? "Sir, I don't know what she told you, but—"

Applegate scowled and pointed the duck at him. "Don't ya get smart with me. I was purdy good with my hands when I wuz your age, and I'd hate ta have to get up thar and shame you—"

Will couldn't quite grasp the picture of Applegate taking a swing at him. "Sir, I don't know what's got you so riled up, but I assure you that I didn't mean to do anything to upset you like this."

"'Tain't me that I'm worried about. It's my Haley Bell. You need to apologize, and I mean good."

Will let out a long breath and kept his mouth shut instead of pointing out that was exactly what he'd come to do. But this was between him and Haley, and he wasn't going to let Applegate intimidate him into letting him in on what was going on. If Haley wanted to tell the world her business, that was her choice. He chose not to.

"Sir, if you could just let me know where she is."

"She went out on her horse fer a spell."

"Her horse." Will glanced toward the barn.

"Yer welcome to take one of the other horses out if you had a mind to do such a thing. They could use the exercise."

Will brightened. "I think I'll do that, sir. Is there a certain one—"

"Muffin could use a ride." Applegate lifted a brow. "If you can handle him. He's a bit ornery."

Will hid a smile, remembering the big black and how Haley always had given her animals cutesy names. "I think I can handle him, sir."

Applegate shrugged. "Okay, have at him. He's the black."

"I remember, sir," Will said, tipping his hat in respect for Haley's grandfather as he headed toward the barn. Applegate always had been protective of Haley. Since he and Birdie had helped raise her, Will didn't blame him. Haley's dad worked on the pipeline, which meant he was on the road most of the time, criss-crossing the country. Haley's mother chose to travel with him and they lived in a large travel trailer, only coming home when work was periodically slow. Because of it, Haley had lived most of the time with Applegate and Birdie. So the older man had a right to be protective of his granddaughter. Will was pretty certain if he ever had any kids, especially little girls, he'd be a boyfriend's worst nightmare. Of course, he wasn't

Haley's boyfriend anymore. But he didn't think it appropriate to point that out to App.

It didn't take Will long to saddle the big black and head out. There hadn't been any reason to ask which way Haley had ridden out. After this long an absence from Mule Hollow, there was only one direction she'd have gone—toward the river. Haley always loved the river, and she and Will spent many hours riding the trails that followed along its peaceful banks. Back then Muffin had been a spunky two-year-old, and Puddin, Haley's favorite horse, hadn't been much older. The two horses loved to run as much as he and Haley had loved being together, riding with the wind in their hair and their love in the air.

It had been their favorite date.

Will's mood soured thinking about it, wondering how all of that could have been such a lie. He'd spent some long nights raging at the Lord about it, and he'd come away with little satisfaction. Eventually he'd just let it go…. God's plans were God's plans, and he and Haley as one obviously wasn't part of them.

Still, riding into the woods, he could almost hear her laughter and see her on Puddin, riding out ahead of him. "I need a hand here," Will said out loud, looking up toward the sky, searching for some sign from the Lord that he was going to get a little support in the awkward situation.

But it was a clear sky, and Will didn't feel any kind of support.

It was as Miss Adela was fond of saying, "God was God. He does what He wants and watches how we respond to His actions."

Will figured if that were so, then the Lord was probably not too happy with him right now.

Will figured that just made them even.

Chapter Nine

Haley hadn't been on a horse in ten years, but it was like riding a bicycle. When she'd climbed onto Puddin's back, she'd felt an excitement she hadn't experienced in years. She hadn't realized how much she'd missed riding every day. Of course, tomorrow her sore legs would remind her just how long it had been since she'd been in the saddle. The pain would be worth it, though, because riding always had been a way for her to relax and unwind. She did some of her best thinking while riding, and she needed stress relief as she'd never needed it before. She'd acted like a child.

What had she been thinking? Stomping out like that—*ohhhh* how she hated to apologize for anything. She always had. She was stubborn when it came to backtracking. And now, just look at the situation she'd put herself into. If she'd just kept her cool, held her tongue and talked about production props, she'd have been fine.

Then talking to Applegate, well that had been like a big fat slam to her conscience. How could she have left him here all this time and not come home to check on him? Was she one of those people who forgot about her responsibility to the people who loved her? Who just walked away? It was a hard fact to face about herself...and she needed to think.

Sensing it, Applegate had told her that he'd stashed in the hall closet a big box of clothes she'd left behind. She hadn't wasted any time dragging it out. Sure enough, there was a box of her old jeans, some T-shirts and a couple of pairs of boots. One of them was her favorite pair, soft and worn and as comfortable as slippers. Elated, she'd changed clothes, thrilled that she could actually fit into the jeans. Of course, her figure had shifted a bit and they were a little tighter than she remembered them being ten years earlier, but she wasn't complaining. She'd quickly pulled on her boots and coat, then hurried to the barn and saddled up her horse, Sweet Puddin. Funny how she'd let something she loved so much slip away, but keeping up with the fast-paced real-estate market of Beverly Hills hadn't left much room for horses.

Her job hadn't left much room for anything except business—racing to make the next big sale. She had a bank account to prove that she was successful at her job, but what else?

She pushed away the thoughts, breathed in the cool crisp air, and took the eastern path. It was purely out of old habit that she rode the familiar trail. She'd created this trail as a child, and memories bombarded her as she rode. Memories of her and Will loping on horseback came immediately to mind. The man wouldn't leave her alone. He was everywhere. She paused where the trail snaked through the woods to the river.

Sitting in the saddle now, she pushed the sound of his laughter out of her thoughts and studied first the path to the left that would lead her downstream along the edge of the woods then circle back around to Gramps's house again. Then she studied the trail that would take her deeper into the woods before coming out farther upstream. It was that trail she chose despite the pain she knew she would suffer tomorrow for pushing herself her first day back in the saddle.

She'd gone pretty deep into the woods when she paused on the trail. She was pushing a tree branch out of her way when suddenly a squeal broke through the silence and a wild baby boar charged from the underbrush. One minute Haley was in the saddle, the next she was flying toward the ground with one thing on her mind—where there was a baby boar, a mean mama boar was somewhere near.

Scenes from *Old Yeller* flashed through her mind, reminding her that the ground was not a place she needed to be when a tusked wild sow bent on protecting its young came around the corner.

Haley hit the ground with a thud that rattled her brains but thankfully didn't knock the breath out of her. This was a good thing because she could see the bushes moving and the ground shaking. That meant only one thing—something mean, mad and ugly was coming her way!

Haley scrambled to her knees just in time to see the female bush hog charging toward her like a linebacker on the tackle. Like all wild hogs, it was pure lean muscle with blackish bristles and two sharp, destructive tusks curving up beside its prominently extended snout. A snout that was about the ugliest thing Haley had ever seen. Anyone who'd grown up in Texas knew that wild boars were fearsome would-be killers when cornered. As mean as they were ugly.

Haley knew all of this.

"Wh-whoa, girl," she managed to say, scrambling up, knowing her only defense was to run. On her feet at last, she dove hard to the right as the queen of ugly missed her by a hair. Boars were agile, and Her Ugliness proved it when she twisted around, sharp tusks glistening in the light, and came immediately back at Haley. Gasping, Haley grabbed a broken tree branch, thinking that maybe if a boar had a weak spot she could buy herself a little bit of time by smacking it on its nose or something. She said a prayer as it was charging straight at her. She barely had time to swing the limb like a baseball bat.

It connected with the boar's thick skin with a jarring impact that sent Haley stumbling back while the pig came to a dead halt, shook its head and thought about what had just happened to it. It decided within a matter of a split second that it didn't much appreciate getting smacked on the jaw by a human. Madder than ever, it lifted its head, met Haley's gaze, then charged again. This time it emitted an unearthly sound that would have scared the life out of a person with much more courage than Haley had. Haley screamed like the girl she was and resumed running.

Okay, so she really admired that men could control their vocal cords when it came to screaming—and she readily admitted that she despised squealing—but the thing was, she wasn't a man and this repulsive heap of bad pork chops was about to shred her like cedar logs thrown in a mulch machine! She opened up her vocal cords and continued to let 'em rip. She was being chased by a pig. A pig with sharp tusks and slobber-covered teeth that liked to eat anything and everything. Why, Haley would simply be a delicacy to a pig like this!

Heart pounding, feet, too, she scanned the woods as branches slapped at her, and her options raced through her brain. She was a great problem solver, but this, *this* was a little out of her league. She was seconds from being mowed down when she saw the hog trap.

It was your standard hog trap, about four feet tall and five feet long, sitting on the edge of the woods waiting for an unsuspecting hog. Haley wasn't the hog, but she saw protection and without hesitation charged inside, instantly tripping the trap door. As the heavy guillotine-style cage door slid down behind her with a bang, Haley almost passed out from relief. Especially when the Queen of Ugly rammed the door with the force of a bull.

The force knocked Haley off her feet and sent her tumbling into the far wall of the cage. Madder than ever, the pig squealed and started rooting around the edge of the cage, glaring at Haley through the metal. Haley nervously studied the bars and wondered exactly how safe she was. She reassured herself that Applegate wouldn't put a cheap cage out, so she calmed down. She was safe.

Thank goodness it didn't take the pig long to grow bored with her or get a headache from ramming the cage with its head. Haley breathed a sigh of relief watching it disappear into the woods.

"What a day," she mumbled when the last

sound of rustling leaves died away. Hunkered down inside the cage, she studied her now peaceful surroundings. It wasn't exactly the tranquility she'd envisioned when she'd saddled up Puddin.

She listened for the pig but figured it was long gone. Still, she wasn't certain she was ready to leave the safety of the cage, not just yet. Instead, she wrapped her fingers around the bars and couldn't help laughing at the picture she must make.

Just a few days ago she'd been dressed in a designer wedding gown, and now she was inside a cage in the middle of nowhere looking like a monkey at the zoo.

Deciding it was better that no one saw her or ever heard about this, she crawled over to the door and reached for the latch. But it looked funny.

It looked broken.

She groaned, tried to pull the hinge, but the lever had jammed, probably from the impact of the pig ramming into it. After a moment of working with it, she realized there was nothing she could do to release the mechanism.

Haley's heart sank. She was trapped inside a cage.

A pig cage.

This would not do. This would not do at all.

Grabbing the bars with both hands, she shook them. But that was about as effective as a spider monkey trying to shake free of a heavy iron leash.

Applegate had never been one to do a job halfway, and he'd obviously bought a cage that would hold a rhino-size hog.

Haley was stuck in the hog trap.

It was a Haley Bell story that would rival the best of them. And with the way her luck was going, an early ice storm would blow in and freeze her to the bars.

Miserable, Haley sank to the floor and looked gloomily out at her surroundings. At this point, getting frozen like an ice cube might be the only bright spot in an otherwise pathetic day.

Chapter Ten

There were too many memories creeping out of the woods to haunt Will as he rode out to find Haley.

He'd spent hours traipsing through these woods, hunting and fishing.

And riding with Haley.

At the fork in the trail, he took the one that wound deeper into the woods. The woods were dense here, but would eventually open up to a small cove where Haley loved to sit and think. Yet he hadn't gone far when he saw her horse. Alarm rang through Will at the sight of Puddin's empty saddle.

"Haley," he called and rode toward Puddin. When no answer came, he scanned the bushes and searched the trail for signs of her. The woods were silent as he called again, but still no reply. He hurried forward. Every terrible scenario he could imagine rose in his mind. She could have fallen and could be lying somewhere hurt; she wouldn't let her horse wander around if she was okay. And she would have answered him. Forcing down the fear, he urged his horse forward, toward the river. He hadn't gone ten feet when he saw where she'd fallen from her horse. His alarm increased when he saw the hog tracks. He knew how to track, but it didn't take much to see that a scuffle had happened here. Hurrying he followed her trail through the woods, toward the rushing water where the river bottlenecked through a rocky area before pooling upstream around the bend. He was praying that the loud sound of the rapids were making it hard for her to hear his calls for her as he urged Muffin on as fast as he dared on the uneven terrain.

Hogs were mean and could shred anything that got in their way if they were mad enough or scared enough. If Haley had fallen in the path then he hated to think what he would find upstream, the fact that he wasn't seeing blood gave him hope. He bent low to miss a pine tree branch. And then he saw her slumped inside the large hog pen near the edge of the woods.

Anyone other than Haley he would have been startled to see in a hog pen, but for Haley it fit. Another escapade for her long list. However, he wasn't focused on that as he sprang from the saddle. "Haley," he called.

"Oh, Will," she said the moment she saw him. "Am I glad to see you."

He took in the tracks around the pen, evidence that the hog had tried to get at her even after she'd made it into the protection of the heavy metal pen. It had been smart thinking on her part but why was she still inside?

"I was hiding from a hog and the latch broke. Who ever heard of a latch breaking?"

Will smiled at the relief in her voice and immediately went about getting her out of the trap. He pulled out his pocketknife and after a minute was able to open the latch and raise the door.

Without any urging, Haley scrambled out, smiling in relief. "Free at last! Whew, I am just a little too tall for that cage."

Will chuckled, all the tension between them forgotten momentarily. "I'm glad you found it. Didn't Applegate tell you he was trying to trap a wild hog?"

Haley waved the question away. "Will, you know as long as I can remember my grandpa has been trapping hogs. It's the only way to keep them under control and not let them take over his land. You know that old saying he's always quoting, that 'If a wild hog has six piglets you can expect eight to survive.'"

That was almost true. The animals populated faster than people could trap them and haul them away. For the most part they let people be, but they could ruin a man's property if left to their own devices. "So what happened?"

"Me and Puddin startled a baby and Puddin reared up and I slid right off into the path of a protective mama. She was just defending her baby. I would have done the same thing if I was in her position."

Will couldn't stop staring at her. She was beaming from excitement. She looked fresh and young, and it suddenly hit him that she was wearing her favorite orange T-shirt beneath her jacket. He remembered it because he had a picture of her in that same shirt in his wallet all through college. He took a step back at the memory as it threatened to open a floodgate of emotions. The memories were too painful to think about because of the promise they'd held and the loss they now represented.

"What are you doing here?"

Her question jarred him and he lifted his gaze from the shirt. "I came to talk and after Applegate gave me the once-over, he told me you were riding and let me borrow Muffin to come find you."

Her face softened. "I am so glad you showed up."

They stared at each other for a long moment. Will didn't know what she was thinking, but he was having a hard time not thinking about all the times they'd stood beside this river and shared kisses.

He cleared his throat. "Yeah, well, me, too."

Haley blushed and he realized that maybe she'd been thinking about the same things he'd been thinking.

"After the way I acted at your house, I'm surprised you came." She tucked her hands into her back pockets and looked at him with clear green eyes.

He cleared his throat again. "Look, Haley, I've been sarcastic ever since you showed up here and while I don't pretend that we can go back and change whatever it was that went wrong between us, I do think we should at least make an effort to work together. I mean, we are adults."

She didn't say anything but he could tell her mind was whirring. Her eyes had always brightened, grown sharper when she was wading through things. Will always had admired her thinking process. He wondered suddenly if he'd ever told her that. The realization that he couldn't ever remember telling her how much he liked the way her mind worked caused him to wonder if she'd noticed. Of course she had. He felt uncomfortable now at discovering his lack of consideration.

"You're right," she said a heartbeat later. "I actually came out here to think." She scanned the surroundings. "The way I see it, despite our past we should still be able to conduct ourselves in an adult manner. I mean, we are both businesspeople, after all. We know what it takes to relate to people without getting personal so we should be able to put our differences aside and move forward."

Businesspeople—Will's temper flared at the thought that she wanted to treat him like a mere business acquaintance. It was irrational on his part, especially in light of this new revelation.

"Right," he snapped in a completely non-businesslike response. *Right?* What kind of an answer was that? He raked his hat off his head with his right hand and ran the fingers of his left hand through his hair. He studied her for a long moment, half expecting her to smile and say she was joking. But she wasn't and he knew it. He should be apologizing to her for not expressing enough admiration all those years ago. But what did it matter now?

Where was the Haley he'd loved? Moments ago when he'd come upon her stuck in the hog trap, he'd glimpsed his Haley. The one who was always getting herself into funny escapades that he needed to rescue her from. He realized now that for a brief moment he'd hoped, however unrealistic a thought it was, that they had a chance of getting back together. But he'd been dreaming…or *hallucinating* might be the better word because this woman who looked at him as only a fellow *businessperson* had no interest in anything of the sort. What had he been thinking?

Haley looked around for the boar, knowing that it was long gone but needing something other than Will to occupy her thoughts. Taking a deep breath, she tugged her coat tighter, feeling the temperature drop even though it was midafternoon. It was going to be a cold Thanksgiving, which was nice. Although she hated cold weather, there was just something about a brisk Thanksgiving Day that made it feel more traditional.

Haley was hit by the irony of her situation. A few days ago she'd almost married one of the wealthiest men in the United States. She'd walked away in search of something that she couldn't put a finger on, and today she was crawling out of a pigpen nearly on her hands and knees feeling like a skunk rather than a free woman. It was true. She was a mess and Will Sutton wasn't helping the situation in any way, shape, or form. Standing tall, methodically thumping his black Stetson against his thigh, she was so tempted to ask him if he'd ever thought about what it would have been like if they'd gotten married that day.

Haley blinked hard and came to her senses.

What was she thinking? Did she want more humiliation?

She'd just told him they should be able to conduct themselves in an adult manner, and she was about to bring up the past. Well, it was time to get over it.

"Anyway, I'll help with the design of the props and I won't have any more childish outbursts. Is that a deal?"

She held out her hand. It was a normal thing to do. She shook hands in her business ten, sometimes twenty times a day. Shaking hands was a natural extension of the type of relationship she was trying to set up between her and Will.

His jaw clenched slightly, drawing her gaze. And then he reached out and grasped her hand in a brief, firm handshake.

"You're right," he said, his eyes cool. "We're adults, after all."

Haley nodded, her gaze dropping to the impersonal handshake.

Yes, they were adults.

So she reminded herself again to act like one.

"Haley! Yoo-hoo, Haley!"

Hearing her name yelled out, Haley stopped outside of Sam's and searched the length of Main Street. Down the street at Heavenly Inspirations, Esther Mae was waving furiously. Haley waved back.

"Come down here," Esther Mae shouted.

With nothing pressing other than grabbing

a soda and watching Applegate and Stanley battle it out over their checker game before she headed out to Will's, Haley easily changed course. Crossing the street, she strode down the sidewalk past several vacant buildings, past a candy store that looked interesting, past the dress store she'd yet to venture into, and finally to the glaring pink two-story building that housed Heavenly Inspirations. Up close, it was even pinker than she'd thought—if that was possible.

Esther Mae, her hair in white perm rods outlined with a thick strip of cotton and topped off with a clear processing cap, waved her forward. She stank like the perm she was getting—like rotten eggs and Haley felt sorry for her poor husband, Hank. He'd have to be in the same house with her for the next few days until the scent wore off.

"We were just talking about you and then, 'ta-da!' You drive up. Imagine that. I was standing right there in the doorway—had to because I can't stand the smell of these perms, they're worse smelling than an auction barn on sale day…if you know what I mean. But, I was in the mood for a little pick-me-up so Lacy's fixing me up. Like my mama always said, a girl has to suffer to be beautiful. Hey, everyone, look who's here," she bellowed suddenly and then basically yanked Haley inside and blocked her escape.

The salon was packed. Norma Sue was getting a trim, but Lacy paused long enough to whip over and give Haley a hug. Though they'd only just met, Haley felt a kinship with Lacy that she didn't quite understand. If her instincts were on target, Lacy felt it, too.

"We are so glad you came in," Lacy exclaimed and everyone echoed her welcome. There was Esther Mae and Norma Sue, then Adela and Sheri, the nail tech she'd met at the theater meeting.

"I've been hoping to get to know you a little better," Lacy said. "I feel almost like a kindred spirit with you already." She laughed as she took her place behind the styling chair and started snipping at Norma Sue's wiry gray hair. "We sound like we have a lot in common. Have a seat over there." She pointed the scissors at the empty hair-dryer chair.

Haley backed up and sat down. "We do?" she asked, curious, but not at all surprised that Lacy had heard stories.

Chuckles erupted around the room. Lacy paused her scissors in midair and grinned at

Haley. "From what I've heard from Applegate over the last few days, you have a habit of acting on things before you've thought them through all the way."

Haley smiled weakly and shrugged. "Guilty as charged. But I've gotten better over the years."

Lacy turned serious suddenly, dropping the section of curly gray hair, her penetrating blue eyes seeming to peer into Haley's soul. "Why did you have to get better?"

Haley was taken aback by the intensity of the question as all eyes turned toward her. "Well, I—" she stumbled over her response. "Crazy spontaneity with a tendency toward screwups isn't exactly the way to advance a career. Or to get taken seriously," she added, deciding to be totally honest.

Lacy chuckled, pointing the hot-pink comb she held. "The way I've always looked at it is if I couldn't be myself, then I wasn't being honest."

Sheri hooted from the corner. "She has to say that or she'd get herself in trouble. Lacy couldn't be any different even if she tried."

"And we wouldn't want her to be," Adela said in her soft voice. Always the mediator, calm, cool and collected.

"And I agree," Sheri said, bending over Adela's nails as she added a blush-pink to them. "I was just letting Haley in on what we all know, but she hasn't had a chance to realize."

Haley managed a smile. "Well, I've been reading Molly's newspaper column."

"Oh," Norma Sue said, meeting Haley's gaze in the reflection of the mirror, since her back was to Haley. "So you've been reading all about us. Is that why you dropped that fella and came home? You realized since we have things going on around here that you might actually want to settle down here at last."

Haley had to give them credit for laying things out in the open. "I said I was reading the articles. But I didn't marry Lincoln because it wasn't right, and I realized it just in the nick of time. He knew it, too—"

"So, how are the set designs going?" Lacy asked, abruptly changing the subject.

"Um, good. I'm actually on my way out to Will's this morning to start. We had our first meeting yesterday."

"Oh, really," Esther Mae cooed, fanning herself with a magazine from the open doorway. "Did y'all make any progress?"

Haley got the feeling the question didn't exactly pertain to the props. She ignored the insinuation. "A little. We'll do better today." She hoped.

Esther Mae grinned at Norma Sue then at Haley. "That's what we're hoping for."

Haley bit her lip. If they wanted to have these unfortunate ideas, she couldn't do anything to dissuade them, but she had no illusions. "Well, I need to go. I was just swinging by the diner to tell Applegate good morning. I swear that man rises before the chickens. Y'all must, too, since you already set all those rods in Esther Mae's hair."

"Well, you know what they say, the early bird gets the perm," Esther Mae said, grinning. "And we've got a lot of costume sewing to do."

Haley made a face. "Glad that's y'all and not me."

Norma Sue chuckled. "We are, too. We remember how bad you were at that. Birdie tried, though."

Haley laughed. "Yes, she did. But it just didn't take."

"It sure was entertaining, though," Esther Mae said.

Haley paused at the door, said her

goodbyes and left the salon. She realized as she walked down the sidewalk that she'd enjoyed the visit.

She was enjoying the majority of her stay in Mule Hollow. For a place she'd been glad to leave behind, she was beginning to think the tiny community might have possibilities she'd missed. Yet there was all that small-town meddling…. *Caring* would be more a way the ladies would look at the hopes they seemed to harbor for her and Will.

Though their *caring* was touching, it was also worrisome. Still, she couldn't help thinking that Mule Hollow's charm was beginning to draw her in like a magnet.

Down at the diner, Applegate, Stanley and Sam were deep in conversation as they peered through the front window watching Haley leave Heavenly Inspirations.

"She looks happy ta me, App," Stanley said, popping a couple of sunflower seeds into his mouth.

"Yup," Sam agreed. "Looky how content her face is right now. I think you might be right about this, Applegate. This 'Operation: Married by Christmas' plan of yorn might just have a chance."

Applegate watched his granddaughter climb into her car and said yet another prayer that the good Lord would give him his Christmas wish…for Haley's sake. "I ain't one to ask fer much, but I figure the Lord already has plans fer my Haley girl and Will. If I'm right, then alls it's gonna take is us puttin' them in the same vicinity and nature will take its course."

Stanley scratched his nose and studied Applegate. "I hope yer right, App. But even though they was supposed to get married ten years ago a week before Christmas don't mean they got any sentimental value to the date all these years later. I know yor hoping that'll play inta this, but it might not happen."

Applegate sat up straight from the checkerboard and glared at his friend. "So what're ya saying? I should jest give up?"

Sam raised his hands. "Calm down, you old fool. No need to get riled. Stanley and me just don't want you to get yer hopes up too high. No, now don't look at me that way. We thank those two could have a chance if they could figure out what's blocking thar way. But we jest don't want you ta have a conniption if it don't work out."

Applegate watched Haley's car disappear

down Main Street before leveling determined eyes on his longtime buddies. "This is gonna work. Mark my words. With all of us doin' our parts, we're havin' a wedding come Christmas. I got a good feelin' about this."

Stanley frowned at him. "Yep, but you had a good feelin' about beatin' me in that last game of checkers, too. And that didn't happen."

Applegate grinned. "But it's fixin' to. Set that board up, and let's see who wins this next game. I'm feelin' lucky."

Haley and Will, by mutual silent agreement, put their differences aside and set out to get the props designed. There were several scenes that needed to be drawn out before any painting could be done. For the next three days Haley showed up, and she and Will sketched. It bothered her being around him, but she concentrated on the work and ignored the strange unwanted feelings that ran like an underground river beneath the surface of her skin.

On Sunday Haley went to church with Applegate. He basically showed her off, acting so proud to have her there that once again

Haley felt glaringly embarrassed by her absence from his life.

She was also embarrassed that she hadn't set foot inside a church since attending her grandmother's funeral. She sat on the back row beside Applegate and felt as if God was tapping her on the shoulder through the entire service. Though she could have been uncomfortable, she wasn't. Since leaving Mule Hollow, she'd felt as if she were running on fast forward, determined to get somewhere quickly. But when she'd left Linc at the altar and turned her car toward her hometown, she'd started a journey. Maybe, sitting here in this pew, letting her heart hear a gentle knock of the Lord, was where she'd been heading the whole time.

Monday morning Haley woke up thinking about the service and one of the key verses Pastor Allen had preached on: *Be still and know that I am God.* It had been a long time since she'd actually thought about giving God her time. In the quiet of the morning, Haley found herself pulling her grandmother's Bible off the bookshelf in the living room. After padding barefoot back to her bed, snuggled in the folds of her grandmother's quilt, she began to read.

Chapter Eleven

"No, I don't think that looks right," Haley said, leaning her head to the side and gazing critically at the picture she'd just drawn.

Will was standing across from her. He hadn't realized what a perfectionist she'd become until they'd started this project. The scene looked great to him, but he'd learned pretty quickly that Haley wasn't looking to please anyone but herself. Until she was satisfied with the drawing she was making, it wasn't going to do any good for him to try and convince her that she was being too hard on herself.

"Are you this tough to please all the time?"

She bit the pencil she'd been tapping against her chin while she studied the work. "Yes. And I know what you're going to say—I used to be a pushover. I was, but I realized if I wanted to be a success I had to change. So I did."

He'd been standing back getting the full view of the sketch and now he dropped to one knee beside her. "Is that so?"

She flashed him a sassy grin that reminded him of the girl he'd known, and for a moment he almost forgot that they didn't really like each other anymore.

Will grinned back at her. She was different, and it just didn't fit. But what did he know? Over the last few days, she'd been quiet, but so had he. Today, something was different. She'd walked into the workshop earlier and started talking. Though they hadn't, until this moment, talked about anything remotely personal. She'd asked all about Mule Hollow and his work. She seemed genuinely interested.

However, he noticed that she was careful not to ask him why he'd left Mule Hollow in the first place. After all, before she'd walked away from him, he'd planned to live in Mule Hollow. It was the main reason she'd left. But her leaving him had changed his plans. Unable to face all the memories and being pitied by everyone, he'd taken a job with a

Dallas architecture firm owned by a couple of his college buddies. Haley Bell Thornton had no idea how badly she'd torn his world apart. Relentlessly, her memories held and followed him everywhere he'd moved.

Hunkered down beside her on the cold concrete, he got lost staring at her profile as she scrutinized the large sketch. Aware he was in a danger zone, he forced his gaze to the drawing. "It looks…" his eyes were drawn back to her "…good. But then I didn't see anything wrong with it in the first place." He itched to touch her, suddenly wanting to trace his finger along her jaw. Instead he curled his fingers into a fist and pressed it into the floor.

Unaware of the effect she was having on him, she shook her head, took her pencil and made a new line then erased the first one again.

"Maybe now. Better, don't you think?" She slid a glance at him, her eyes dancing, drawing him like magnets to lean closer.

"Better," he croaked, humoring her while he sprang to his feet and moved away from her as fast as he could. What was the matter with him? Just because she'd come in today with less of a chip on her shoulder and the desire to talk didn't mean anything had changed. He was a fool for letting his emotions conquer his resolve.

"Will," she said softly, her tone causing his step to falter. "Will, what happened to us?"

Her question took him by surprise. So much so that he almost blurted out that he didn't have a clue, except that her vision of fortune had lured her away.

"I mean," she chuckled suddenly. "It's like now I'm you and you're me. I used to be the haphazard, abstract one and you were the toe-the-line, everything-had-to-be-just-so guy."

Will almost laughed at the irony. He'd thought she was talking about them as a couple and she'd meant as people in general. With space between them, he considered her thoughtfully for a moment, then lifted a shoulder. What could he say? "Like you said, people change."

"I've always been fascinated by the why of it though. What makes a person make the change?"

Will had started walking to his welding machine, but her words stopped him in his tracks. It was such a familiar thought for him. He'd had the exact same thought only moments before. People changed when forced. He spun on his heel and studied her…then changed the subject.

"Do you want to see the finished bridge?" *Way to go, Sutton. Real clever thing to say when she's just blown your socks off with a revelation about herself that hits home with you.*

"Actually, I would love to see the bridge."

"Then follow me. It's out back."

He led the way outside his workshop to a covered-but-open area where he kept his steel rods and scrap metal and wood. He'd set the small bridge in the center of the work space.

"It looks pretty rugged right now."

Haley walked around the five-foot-long bridge, studying it intently. When they finished, it would sit in front of a painting that made it look as if it crossed a rushing river.

"When it's all put together this is going to look pretty impressive," she said, running her fingers across the wood. "You are a handy guy. No wonder they wanted you to get involved." She met his gaze across the bridge, the corner of her lips curling into a half smile. "Imagine if I tried to build this."

Will looked away from her as old feelings

stirred to life. Disturbed by the force of his emotions, he walked to the edge of the building and stared out at the cows grazing across the fence in his pasture. Working with Haley was proving to be harder for him than he'd ever expected. Having to stand near her was torture. The ever-so-light sweet scent that seemed to cling to her skin and hair whispered for him to lean closer, to inhale deeper…but that was only the surface. It was Haley herself that was getting to him.

"Have you read any of the script?" he asked, running a hand down his face, grasping at conversation.

She came to stand beside him, laying a hand against the steel pole extending to the metal roof.

"Yes, I've read it. It's a bit of a twist, looking at how Mary and Joseph affected the people around them as they stepped up and prepared to live out the life God destined for them. In giving God control, they fulfilled their purpose. I like the way Lacy is using the play to ask the audience if we're fulfilling our purpose."

Will let his gaze drop to the ground but didn't say anything. He was at a loss for what his purpose was.

Haley tucked her hands into the pockets of her coat and took a deep breath. "About the time I got engaged to Linc, I started asking the big questions—that one included. So imagine my surprise to come here and get pulled into a production focusing on stepping up to fulfill your destiny."

"What was it about this Linc guy that made you start thinking about it?" He wanted to ask what was different about running out on groom number three versus running out on him. But he held back.

She looked straight at him. "It was simple. I sold my first multimillion-dollar property that day. What a feeling that was. I was already making great money prior to that, but that was a real milestone. I was ecstatic, yet I felt empty inside. Linc had been after me for months to marry him, and that day I said yes. The thoughts started then. Almost immediately. I know this sounds horrible, but I woke up the next morning thinking that I had achieved my career goals. I'd made it. I was someone, plus I'd achieved a wedding proposal from a lovely, rich man who respected who I was, my success, my brains—but I felt empty. And I couldn't figure out why that was. I was on top of the world, yet I was so sad."

Will crossed his arms over his chest, anger taking over. "So, is that your reasoning behind walking away from groom number three? I mean, you walked away from me to find fame and fortune, and you walked away from him because it wasn't enough? What about groom two? I'm sure it was something similar."

She narrowed her now fierce eyes at him. "You really are a jerk. You know that, Sutton?"

"Me?" The woman was a piece of work.

She crossed her arms and cocked her head to the side. "Yes, you. How could you say I walked away from you to find fame and fortune? You still don't see that that wasn't it at all. I can't believe you would think that. Wait. It all comes down to the same thing— you never heard me. Never cared about what *I* needed."

"I heard you plenty. What was I supposed to think? We planned to get married, then suddenly all you could talk about was how no one respected you and you were going to make it big some day—"

"Whoa." She held up a hand and glared at him. "I didn't talk about it all the time. I was just frustrated to always have everyone think I was nothing but a klutz. How would you like it if everyone all the time told stories about your mishaps? If everyone made fun of you all the time and didn't take you seriously?"

"That's not the way it was."

Her mouth dropped open and her eyes widened. "That was exactly how it was. You were one of the worst."

It was his mouth that dropped open this time as he tightened his crossed arms and shifted his weight to one hip. "That is not so. Not so at all. How could you even think that?"

She slammed her hands to her hips. "And how exactly do you remember it? I walked up on you numerous times telling stories about me. Like—" she looked out at the cows, thinking, and then back at him "—like the time you were telling all the guys out front of Pete's about how I was helping you clean out your daddy's barn and I slipped going up the ladder to the hayloft and my coat snagged on that protruding board. You even compared me to a side of beef hanging in a meat cooler. Flapping my arms like I was trying to fly. Those were your exact words."

"I didn't—"

"Don't even try to deny it. I remember.

When someone says something that hurts you, believe me, you don't forget it. And that wasn't the only time. Like the time I ordered milk at Sam's and you asked me if I wanted pasteurized or unpasteurized, and I said either one was fine with me... Just because I didn't realize that all milk sold in a store was pasteurized didn't mean I was stupid. It just meant I never thought about it before. But, you—you had to go tell all your friends and for years every time I asked for milk someone asked me if I wanted pasteurized or unpasteurized."

He started chuckling despite the anger knotting his gut together. She had him all wrong. He wasn't the kind of guy to make fun of someone. "Haley, come on. That was not what I meant and you know it—"

She held up a hand. "No. You let me finish. You never took me seriously. When I told you I wanted to get my real-estate license, you told me that contract negotiations were intricate. *Intricate!* Like I was too dumb to understand how to read a contract."

Will took a deep breath. "Haley, I told those stories because I thought they were cute."

"Cute!" she exclaimed.

Glaring at him, she blinked hard, her eyes

bright—was she near tears? "I didn't mean—" His anger dissipated. He'd rarely seen Haley cry.

"Did it ever occur to you that I might want to be more than cute? That I might need the man who was supposed to love me to have faith in me? Look, I've got to go."

Stunned by her outburst, Will watched her leave. Women! He was beginning to think there was a good reason he was still single. He just didn't understand women.

Particularly Haley Bell Thornton.

Chapter Twelve

Why had she said all that to him? She sounded like a crybaby. That had all happened so long ago. How could it even matter…

She wasn't that woman anymore. What was wrong with her?

She started reading her Bible the night before; she even prayed. She felt so good this morning…but that Will Sutton.

Ohhh, the man! He was just irritating.

And to think they'd actually been getting along. Of course, they'd both been careful to stay away from anything remotely personal. But still, they'd been starting to renew their friendship. Okay, that was stretching it. But there had been moments when she'd looked at him and let herself think about what her life would be like today if she'd chosen not to leave Mule Hollow.

If she'd stayed and married Will.

Stomping on the brake, Haley slung rocks as she brought her Beamer to a halt at the end of Will's drive. Distraught, she dropped her forehead to her hands, which were clutching the steering wheel as if it were a life preserver and she was sinking in choppy waters. Of all the ways she'd wanted him to see her, a whining, weak woman…a bitter woman was not one of them. Oh, how could she have let her guard down like that?

Sucking in deep breaths, Haley asked God to calm her. Of course, she knew good and well she'd messed up and that God was probably disgusted with her.

She rested her chin on her hands and stared blankly through the windshield as she fought the urge to go back and tell Will she was sorry for her outburst. But she couldn't seem to wrap her mind around that idea.

So she just sat there, motor running, with her entire life in limbo. Her gaze settled on the abandoned home across the street in front of her. It looked as lost and forlorn as she felt.

Haley had been born interested in real estate. She always thought it was funny to think back to kindergarten when the teacher had asked each of her classmates what they wanted to be when they grew up. Haley had sat in a typical group of aspiring teachers, lawyers, firefighters and doctors. Then it had been Haley's turn. Haley, who'd blurted out without hesitation that she was going to sell houses. Big houses. That had gotten her an uproarious laugh. One of many she would hear over the years.

But here she was all these years later doing exactly what she'd planned. It wasn't rocket science, but it was fun…most of the time. There were those who still thought her chosen profession wasn't what you might call a worthwhile vocation, but it was something that gave Haley joy and she saw it differently. God had given her a good eye for the market and a genuine interest in matching the right property to the right client. Trivial to some, but a house was not trivial. The right house turned into a home, and a home made a connection with its occupants. Like a heartbeat, the right home had a pulse that helped draw families together. Haley had always taken her job very seriously. Although, she'd found the higher the price tag, the less appeal it had for her…and

that might have been part of her problem
of late.

Now, staring at the abandoned home, for-
lornly staring back at her from across the street
with its overgrown yard and crooked shutters,
Haley couldn't stop herself. She needed a
boost, and looking at property was a distraction that drew her and helped soothe her
wounded spirit. Pushing thoughts of Will and
her problems away, she pressed the gas, drove
across the street and up the short drive. She
parked her car, then opened the door and got
out, her shoes crunching on grass-encrusted
gravel. Even after all these years she still got
a thrill when she first looked at property.

There were just so many possibilities. She
loved shows on TV about flipping houses. It
was great to see something old that had been
made new again.

Haley wondered what that would feel like.
But of course you'd have to have a market for
something like that. You'd also have to have
the time. And proximity to the property.
Haley pulled her coat close and walked
toward the run-down house. She didn't have
any of those things, but she could still look.
It was much better than thinking about Will
Sutton.

* * *

Haley had decided to put aside all thoughts of the embarrassing confession she'd made to Will and focus on spending quality time with Applegate. It had taken an afternoon driving around the county exploring property to get her thoughts and emotions back in line. By the time she finished taking some time for herself, she'd felt calmer. She prayed also. She'd been trying to learn to lean on Him more. To ask Him to help her and to guide her. And she'd asked the Lord to help her put everything into perspective. To help her see life through new eyes. Now she was feeling as though maybe God was listening to her.

Finally up to facing Applegate, she arrived home around five and fixed a nice dinner for her granddad. He kept her in stitches the entire time, telling stories about him and Stanley. Haley couldn't help but feel sheepish, really. If a person couldn't laugh at themselves, they were in trouble. Haley could laugh at herself. She could.

Really, she could.

When dinner was done they headed to town to start working on the props for the play.

As they were driving into town she

listened to her grandfather talk. It quickly dawned on her that he didn't enjoy being at home all that much. He liked being in town, seeing people and, of course, stirring things up. Though she'd spoken with him on the phone over the years, there was nothing that could replace actually visiting in person. He got so animated talking about the new life that was being breathed into Mule Hollow ever since Adela, Norma Sue and Esther Mae had come up with their "Revive the Town" campaign that Haley couldn't help but feel it herself. And she was fascinated to realize that beneath the droopy, perpetual frown Applegate wore like a banner, there was the heart of a romantic.

Her gramps a romantic—the thought was mind-blowing. Why, the man had never in all the fifty years he and Birdie had been married brought her a single rose, but it was obvious that he'd done something right. Still, he wasn't your poster boy for the romance department.

However, learning that he'd actually helped get Adela and Sam together was endearing to Haley. Of course he had his own way, hounding poor Sam night and day until Sam had practically had no other recourse *but* to ask Adela to be his wife…something the restaurateur had wanted to do for so long but had feared. Haley just found it endearing that her gramps was a matchmaker. Who'd have ever thought it was possible?

As they entered the full community center, she felt a sense of excitement that she hadn't had up until this moment. She was more relaxed than she'd been since her arrival in town and part of that was due to her earlier embarrassing outburst. Though she'd despised speaking her heart to Will and letting him glimpse the anger that she'd felt about being the laughingstock of Mule Hollow and his part in it, somehow, now that she'd voiced it, she felt free from it. All afternoon as she'd explored abandoned houses, she'd calmed down and felt as if something inside her had shifted. She didn't really know what it was or how to explain it, but it was as if hearing the words spoken out loud had enabled her to look at them objectively. As if maybe God had given her new eyes to see through.

She knew she wasn't the laughingstock of Mule Hollow…. Why, the whole idea was ridiculous. But people had irrational ideas that took hold sometimes and wouldn't let go. The Bible reminded Haley that Satan was a deceiver and a liar. Opening up about it seemed to help flush the irrationality of it all to the surface. All in all, the day had been an eye-opener that Haley recognized she'd needed for some time.

She walked into the building feeling excited about being there and saw that some of the men had helped Will bring their plywood sketches to town, and she was grateful. Not having to face Will alone anymore was a good thing.

"Haley, just the woman I'm looking for. Help!" Lacy called from the front stage. "We need you."

Haley told Applegate that she'd meet him in the back where the props production had been set up. She could see Will already there helping set up the plywood that she'd drawn the scenes on, and there were a few other cowboys opening up paint. It looked as if everything was under control as she weaved her way through the chairs toward Lacy. She might be feeling better, but seeing Will immediately brought back a sense of dread. Still, she had to face him sometime.

"What's up?" she asked, looking up onto the small stage at Lacy.

"Here," Lacy said, handing her a script. "Lilly is playing this role, but her baby,

Joshua, came down with a cold and she didn't want to get him out tonight. So I need a stand-in."

Haley took a step backward. "Isn't there someone else you could get?"

"Sure, but I haven't gotten to spend much time with you, therefore I'm picking you. This way we can get to know each other better."

Haley could have listed a lot of different ways they could spend time together getting acquainted that didn't include exposing her total lack of acting ability. However, Lacy had a way about her that made a person not want to turn her down. Staring at Lacy now, her almost-white hair splashed about her head in erratic curls and her eyes full of such complete enthusiasm for the project she was leading, Haley could find nothing to say except "Where do you need me?"

Okay, so she couldn't act…really. But she didn't have time to get out of it now. And besides, it delayed having to face Will.

Lacy grabbed her by the shoulders, pulled her up onto the stage and pushed her over to a spot beside Bob, Molly's husband. Haley's expression must have been an open book because he took one look at her and chuckled.

"Don't look so shocked. She has that effect on everyone," he said, still chuckling.

Haley smiled faintly, feeling sick. She didn't like being up in front of everyone. Looking around, she swallowed the lump in her throat as she saw people pause what they were doing to watch the action on the stage. Her gaze met Will's and the lump in her throat turned into a knot in her stomach. She forced a smile.

"Relax, Haley," Lacy whispered, dropping her hands from Haley's shoulders, having positioned her where she wanted her.

Haley stood rigidly beside Bob, her smile plastered across her face, and stared at Lacy. "Sure, easy for you to say."

Lacy's eyes twinkled and she winked. "You'll do great. Believe me, I know. All you have to do is read the part of Mary. Come on, relax. We're all friends here."

Haley pushed aside her trepidation, her fake smile relaxing into a real one. Not a big one but a real one. She could do this.

"Haley, did you get that?" Lacy asked.

Haley snapped to at the appeal from Lacy and found that while her mind had wandered, her gaze had settled on Will. He was standing at the back of the room, tool belt slung low on his hips, hands crossed, watching her with an unreadable expression. Probably wondering why she was staring at him.

Shaken, Haley yanked her gaze away from his and focused ón Lacy, who was grinning at her as if she could read her mind.

"Sure," Haley mumbled, then gave up the ghost and admitted she hadn't been listening. "Could you repeat that, please?"

"Love to," Lacy quipped, winking. "Just read the part—don't worry about acting. You're just here for Bob to play his role off of." She paused, waiting for Haley to acknowledge that she got it, and as soon as Haley nodded that she did, Lacy grinned like sunshine, spun around and clapped her hands. "Okay, folks, from the top," she shouted.

Haley's palms were damp and she rubbed them against her jeans, then focused on the words on the page.

"You look good up there, Haley!" Esther Mae exclaimed, halting at the foot of the stage. She was holding a pile of material, had a pincushion wristband on, and a tape measure swung from her neck as she gazed up at Haley. Norma Sue was following her, and she stopped to add her two cents.

"But don't let 'em keep you up there too long," she said, jerking her head in the direction of the props. She couldn't motion with her arms since they were also piled high with material. "All those men back there need a woman to tell 'em what colors to paint what."

"Don't worry," Lacy called. "I'm not going to keep her all night."

Haley saw Lacy wink at them, but since Lacy had already winked at her, she figured that was just part of Lacy's personality. It wasn't until she saw Norma Sue turn sideways, trying to hide her lifted eyebrow from Haley's view, that she knew something else was going on.

They were, after all, the matchmaking force of Mule Hollow. Did they really think there was any matching that needed to be done between her and…Will?

Yeah, right. Haley went back to the script, choosing to ignore their folly. What else could she do? Denial would only dig a hole that would be hard to climb out of. Besides, the way Haley saw it, if they wanted to entertain themselves with thoughts of somehow linking her and Will up again, then who was it going to hurt?

As a matter of fact, it could be interesting. It might even be fun.

Hey, it had been a long roller coaster of a day. She'd come here tonight feeling as though she'd crossed a hurdle that she'd been stumbling over for a decade. And, well, she refused to go backward. She was now on a quest. She was looking for God's plan for her life…and she was also ready to have some fun.

Will slammed his thumb with the hammer, held in a yelp of pain as he dropped the nail and tried to shake off the sting.

"Hey, buddy, if we're ever going to get this prop finished, you're going to have to stop watching Haley."

Will glared at Clint Matlock, who was also nailing a two-by-four onto the back of the prop. He was grinning. "That had to hurt."

"I wasn't—"

Clint shook his head, totally enjoying Will's discomfort. "No use denying it, Will. I've got eyes, too, you know. Me and everyone else on this crew back here. And believe me, I'm not the only one noticing that you can't keep your eyes off that stage. And since I know you're not watching my wife, and she's the only other female up there—" he shrugged "—that makes it pretty obvious who you're staring at."

Will snatched another nail from the bag but refused to admit or deny that he'd been watching Haley. Instead he bashed the nail into the support bar. "Look," he snapped when he was done. "It's not what you're thinking."

"And what exactly would I be thinking?"

Will halted his hammer midswing and shot Clint a look of exasperation. "I'm not going to answer that."

Clint chuckled and leaned closer so that no one else could overhear him. "Will, ask her out."

"What?"

"Hey, don't look at me like that. You know you want to. So do it. Ask her out. You guys never have talked about what happened, have you?"

Will slammed the nail in with two strikes. "Not really. Well, some. She did say that I was mean and inconsiderate. Not those exact words, but you get my drift. The woman walks out on our wedding and then tells me it was my fault. That I was a jerk."

"You gotta admit, there were all those jokes."

"Jokes?"

"Yeah, you know, the Haley Bell stories."

Will let the hammer rest on the plywood and stared blankly at Clint. "I told those stories because she was so cute. I told her that."

"I know that. Look, Will, we were young and stupid. But I've got to tell you. I'm married to about the most impulsive woman God ever created. That Lacy can get into more scrapes. The woman is a walking funny bone. But here's what I know now that I might not have known then—I don't go around telling things on her that I think others will take to the extreme and never let her live down. She trusts me."

She trusts me. Will stared at Clint as his words sank in like hot tar melting into hard pavement. Had Haley trusted him, and he'd unknowingly let her down?

He turned and stared at her. She was laughing at something Bob or Lacy had said. Her head was tilted back, and her shoulders were shaking she was laughing so hard.

He wondered what was so funny and felt a pang of regret that he wasn't in on the joke.

"Clint, I'm a jerk. But that doesn't change

all the facts. There's too much old news between us."

Nate Talbert looked up from where he was painting a tree, at least that's what it was supposed to be, although it resembled more of a bush. "Will, the woman dumped you at the altar. Think before you act. Could you ever trust *her* again?"

Nate was one of the cowboys who hadn't been active in the "Bring Women to Mule Hollow Campaign." But he was a widower and it struck Will as odd that he was talking about not trusting women. Still, Will did not feel comfortable asking him why he thought that way. Will had actually been surprised when he'd offered to help with the production, but thought it was a good sign that the man might be coming around. Then again, maybe not.

Maybe the good Lord had just sent him here tonight to talk sense back into Will's ailing brain.

Chapter Thirteen

Thanksgiving was a big day in Mule Hollow. The church fellowship hall was packed, and Haley watched with mixed emotions as everyone filed in with serving dishes full of food. Obviously, Lacy hadn't heard that Haley had a reputation when it came to handling glass bowls of food because she'd recruited Haley to help get the food organized and set out at the church's Thanksgiving dinner.

It was dangerous work, and Haley was a bit nervous each time she took a bowl from someone.

"Haley Bell, how ya doin today?" Stanley boomed, which suggested his hearing aid was turned down low. He handed her a bowl of green beans but hesitated before he let go of it, giving Haley a look of warning. "You ain't gonna drop it, are you?"

Haley actually laughed. "Don't worry, Stanley, I've got it," she reassured him. Nonetheless, she was extra careful as she took the bowl and braced herself for what she knew was coming.

Stanley looked skeptical watching her hold the dish. Then he glanced at Esther Mae, who was setting another corn casserole beside the other five already on the table. "Esther Mae, you remember the egg-salad fiasco?"

Esther Mae smiled but Stanley kept on talking, not giving her a chance to get a word in.

"You know, when Haley Bell was a little girl and she was helping with the dinner and she dropped the bowl of black-eyed peas?"

Haley knew that practically everyone standing within earshot remembered that little escapade. As all eyes focused on her, she watched Esther Mae's face light with the laugh that was tumbling out of her. "Who could forget that? Haley Bell was so cute trying to catch the bowl of beets. It was beets, Stanley, not black-eyed peas."

"No, it was black-eyed peas that she was

trying to catch," Stanley boomed louder, shaking his head.

"No. It was green-pea salad," Norma Sue chimed in.

"Y'all," Esther Mae huffed, "it was beets that she was trying to catch when she fell into the table. She was so cute when she hit the table and sent all the food flying. Poor Haley Bell was trying so hard to stop the catastrophe from happening and ended up sitting in the middle of all that mess of food with egg salad on her head."

Haley stood holding the bowl of green beans as all eyes turned toward her. Of course they remembered the day. Who would have forgotten it?

She remembered it very well. She'd been ten and trying so hard to do everything right…and then the dish had slipped and, like a house of cards everything had fallen apart. Once again she'd been the cute little Haley Bell, so klutzy—but cute. She was always cute. While everyone had a good laugh, she'd smiled along with them, Haley had been so mortified that she hadn't helped set out the food ever again. And it was beets, by the way, beets that had permanently stained her new dress.

But that was years ago, and if everyone even thought that they'd hurt her feelings it would devastate them.

"I can assure you that will not happen today," Haley laughed, carefully setting the dish on the table. She then took a dramatic step away from the table, drawing more laughter from everyone. It certainly felt good to joke about it now.

"It'd be okay if it did," Norma Sue said, coming up and putting an arm around Haley's waist, squeezing affectionately. "We love our little Haley Bell, always have. Thanksgiving dinners haven't been the same without you here. We've missed you."

Haley placed an arm around Norma's plump shoulders and hugged her back. "And I've missed all of you, too, but I'm still not going to drop egg salad on my head."

Everyone laughed again and Haley did, too. It was funny thinking about it now. Maybe she'd overreacted all those years ago. Enjoying the feeling of being home, she took it all in and caught Will watching her. He met her gaze briefly then turned away, his expression troubled. Haley watched him setting chairs around the extra tables that he and the other men were setting up. She wondered what he was thinking about.

She didn't have time to wonder long as more food came in and Lacy asked her to fill glasses with ice. It was a monotonous job but well out of the way of possible catastrophes so she was happy to help. She'd come a long way from the klutzy little girl, but with all the stories resurfacing, they tended to make her nervous. Growing up she'd been like a gangly colt, all legs and arms. She'd been happy when her body and her motor skills finally caught up with each other. Still, there were times she thought she'd become that girl again. Nerves didn't help. Nerves were dangerous.

Lacy set a pitcher of tea on the table beside the glasses of ice. "I wanted to tell you how much I appreciated you standing in for Lilly the last couple of nights of rehearsal. You've been a real lifesaver—a real cool ladybug," Lacy said, grinning. "But don't worry, Lilly's here today and said she'll be at practice tomorrow night so you're off the hook."

"Whew, you just made my day. Not that I've minded reading for her, but that's just not my talent. As you could tell."

Lacy grinned. "You might be right about

that, but you've really been a great sport about pitching in. I told Will that you'll be able to help him out again with the props, and he seemed glad. I think Applegate might be driving him crazy."

Haley had to slam the brakes on the way her heart sped up at the mention of Will being glad she'd be helping him again. "Applegate has a tendency to do that. I keep telling him he needs to turn his hearing aid up and leave it up. You know how he forgets that he's turned it off."

Lacy's eyes widened in acknowledgment but she opted not to voice her agreement as she filled a glass with tea and set it to the side. For a few minutes they worked silently, Haley filling glasses with ice and Lacy filling them with tea.

"Do you ever think about moving back here, Haley? I mean, your grandfather would really like it. So would the entire town. And—ah—well, others."

Haley let the empty glass she was holding hover above the ice chest as she decided to ignore the "others" comment. "Honestly, I've considered it. But please don't say anything. I wouldn't want to get Applegate's hopes up. Because, Lacy, really, I'm not sure I could do it."

"Any particular reason? Would you like to talk about it?"

Haley shrugged. "You know that saying, 'You can never go home again'?"

Lacy nodded.

"Well, I think in my case it might be true."

"No way!" Lacy set the glass of tea down and laid a hand on Haley's arm. "They *really* love you. And they want what's best for you. I have to tell you that Applegate hasn't had this much spring in his step since the day he marched down Main Street with Sam as he went to ask Adela to marry him. You bring a light into his life that he needs. Goodness, Haley, you bring a light into all of their lives. I've only been a part of everyone's life for a little over a year now, but I've felt like I belonged from the first moment I stepped into town. I'm an outsider, and they've adopted me like I was born and raised here…. But you, you're one of them, you're flesh and bone to these wonderful people. They are so proud of you. Home is only a place you can't go home to if you make it that way."

Proud of her? Haley wasn't so sure about that. "It's not just that, Lacy. I, well, I have a different life in Beverly Hills." How could she tell her that Mule Hollow made her insecure even as it drew her?

"But are you making a difference there? Haley, look at Mule Hollow and what you have to offer."

"I don't know—"

"Then let me put it this way—are you happy in Beverly Hills? Wait, don't answer that, at least not right now. Just think about it."

Haley nodded. "Okay," she said. But she already knew the answer. She wasn't happy in Beverly Hills. She had been coming to that realization for some time now. She knew in her heart she wasn't happy and she hadn't been for a good while.

But what did she do about it? She had serious doubts, even though she loved the people of Mule Hollow, that she could move home. In Beverly Hills she was a respected adult. How could she go from that to being looked at by everyone around her as the child she'd once been?

It was impossible. As much as she loved everyone, she couldn't go back to being that child.

Will found Haley sitting in the children's swing out behind the church. She had her back to him and was gently rocking the swing using the toe of her foot. Her blond hair draped across the side of her face as she held the chain, her cheek resting against her knuckles.

He hadn't liked the conversation he'd heard earlier about the "Haley Bell egg-salad fiasco." It had actually angered him. More at himself than anyone else because it had him questioning his own actions all those years ago.

Had he held Haley back?

"Want a push?" he asked walking up behind her. When she glanced over her shoulder at him, his heart stumbled in his chest.

"Hey, why aren't you eating?" she asked, a smile in her voice. It was the first time they'd been alone since their argument at his house at the first of the week, and he was glad she wasn't still angry.

He grabbed the chain and tugged the swing back. "I felt like I needed some fresh air," he said. Letting the swing go, he watched her hair flutter as she swung forward. He'd always loved her hair.

They remained silent for a few moments as she swung back and forth. Tension coiled inside and after a while Will pulled the swing to a stop. Moving to stand in front of her he was filled with shame.

"I never meant to hurt you."

Haley's eyes turned liquid, then she inhaled, blinked and whatever he'd thought he saw was replaced with a teasing light. "Oh, that—I shouldn't have brought all of that up that day at your home. It was old news. I knew you didn't mean to hurt me. I'm a big girl. I was just mad when I made that silly statement. I never meant—"

Will dropped to one knee. "Haley, I was an idiot. A number-one jerk. How could I have not seen it?"

She sat very still, her eyes liquid pools showing her pain as she blinked hard against threatening tears. "Okay, so it's true. At times, you were," she said softly.

He lifted his hand and traced her jaw, unsure whether she would let him touch her, uncertain if he could handle the feel of her. "I'm beginning to think I was an idiot in more ways than one."

"Will, we were young—"

He shot up and rammed his hands into his pockets to keep from pulling her close. He didn't deserve to touch her. "I wasn't that young. It wouldn't have been an excuse anyway. What kind of a man does that? I loved you, and I was too blind to realize that I was hurting you, disrespecting you every time I told a story about you. I should have been out there taking up for you, and what was I doing? I was leader of the pack when it came to telling stories about you."

Haley rose from the swing and laid her hand on his chest. Her touch felt like it was burning a hole through the fabric of his shirt. "Will, I said all of that in the heat of the moment. It's not like I've been mad all these years about everyone saying those things. They didn't mean anything."

Will didn't believe her. Probably because after he'd heard the egg-salad conversation with wiser ears he felt like such a loser. As endearing as everyone thought it was, looking at it from the point of view of a child growing up with it... Will could only marvel at the sweetness with which Haley had always handled it.

"No, they didn't mean anything by their comments, except that they loved you and thought everything you did was cute and worthy of repeating. But enough is enough."

Haley's expression tensed. "I wouldn't

ruin their fun for the world. If I truly thought they were saying things out of meanness I might, but I know different now. That's part of what made this so confusing."

Will sobered. "Then accept my apologies, anyway. There is no excuse, other than stupidity, for my using you to get a laugh from my buddies."

Haley turned and walked to the edge of the playground. She stood silently for a minute then turned toward him. "Okay, truthfully, I did expect you to stand up for me. But I realize you were blinded by the fact that you, too, thought everything I did was adorable." She rolled her eyes, making a face. "It's my own fault for being so cute. So there, blame my parents. How does that sound?"

Charmed, he laughed and moved to stand in front of her. "You're right about me and everyone thinking you were adorable."

She suddenly grew serious, her eyes shadowed as she studied him. "And that was why I left you at the altar."

What? "I don't understand."

"I know. You didn't then when I tried to explain it, and I don't think you do now. Your lack of realizing that I could be more is what made me understand I couldn't go through with our wedding. Or continue to live in Mule Hollow."

"I never said I didn't think you could be more."

Haley's eyes softened. "You didn't have to say it. No one did. As long as I remained in this town I was handicapped by my cute factor. I didn't stand a chance at becoming who I am today."

Will closed his eyes and knew she spoke the truth.

To an extent.

Chapter Fourteen

The day after Thanksgiving, Will worked tirelessly on the gates he'd been commissioned to finish by Christmas and help with the program. He was going to have to make every minute count, and he still had to squeeze in a quick visit to his parents. What had he been thinking to agree to help with the program?

Not only did he have too much work that needed to be finished, but also he now had to contend with a mind that wouldn't stop thinking about Haley. That was the problem he couldn't deal with.

Setting his protective glasses in place, he picked up his grinder and went to work smoothing out the rough edges of the steel artwork. The monotony of the work helped him think, and he had plenty to think about.

Mainly he was trying to wrap his mind around a way to smooth out the problem that Haley had created for him when she'd walked back into his life.

She wasn't the girl he'd loved all those years ago. She'd grown and evolved into a woman he didn't know. But he was curious about her, as was the entire town. To tell the truth, he was getting more and more irritated with each Haley Bell story. What he used to think of as tales of endearment he was now seeing in another light. And it wasn't pretty. It was taking everything he had in him not to tell everyone to button their lips. Not a good frame of mind to be in, but that was the way he felt. It bothered him that he was so moody when it came to Haley.

She wasn't part of his life anymore and probably never would be. He'd been praying for the Lord to help him deal with the confusion assailing him, but he wasn't getting any peace from it. He knew from experience that God had good reason for not answering his prayers. Still, it didn't mean he was happy about having to be patient waiting for answers.

As a matter of fact, if God didn't do something soon then he might make a move he would regret for the rest of his life. Clint's suggestion to ask Haley out on a date was the worst idea Will had ever heard. But he'd be lying if he didn't admit that a part of him wanted to do exactly that.

Shutting down the grinder, he yanked the safety glasses off and stared unseeingly at the progress he'd made. Despite what she'd told him at lunch, ten years ago Haley had walked out on him, giving him no choice in her decision to leave their dreams behind to pursue her own. He'd be a fool to be drawn to her again. But he was. The thing that scared him more than anything was realizing that if he wasn't careful, he'd find that he wanted her back in his life stronger than he'd ever wanted her…and that was a dangerous thing to admit.

It was an admission that could lead him down a one-way street to another broken heart. That wasn't going to happen again if he could help it.

The question was, could he help it? Every time he was around her, his will, no pun intended, softened.

"Haley, stop kidding around and come back to work."

Haley held the receiver away from her ear

so that Sugar's screeching wouldn't burst her eardrum. She'd come home Friday after working on props and found an urgent message from Sugar waiting on the answering machine. Immediately she called her back even though she would have rather closed the door to her room to contemplate all that was on her mind.

"Calm down, Sugar," she said halfheartedly. "Now, tell me what's got you so wound up."

"Marcus Sims—that's who has me wound up. You said to call if something big came up. Well, this is it. He asked specifically for you. He said that you'd handled the Daltry sale and he wants you to represent him in the sale of his villa. *And* he wants you to help him find new digs. So come home. Do you know what kind of commission that's going to be? And I haven't even mentioned yet that the bosses are getting antsy. Of course, Marcus Sims calling for you was a big blessing from the Man Upstairs—if you know what I'm talking about."

Haley's head was spinning as Sugar talked at warp speed. Marcus Sims calling for her. Haley closed her eyes and pictured the handsome investment manager. She'd met him at one of the benefits where she'd represented her agency, and he'd been a real charmer. So much of a charmer that she'd had to be up front with him almost immediately and let him know she was engaged to Linc. She'd hoped he'd turn some of his charm toward someone else once he knew she was off the market. He'd been charming even then, letting her know if the engagement didn't work out that he'd be back. And now, this sudden urge to sell his home and contract her services? Haley had no illusions; the man knew she'd called off her wedding.

Even though Marcus's calling bothered her for reasons that had nothing to do with selling real estate, his call would work to benefit her by giving her more leverage with her brokers. "Sugar, tell Marcus that I won't be able to do anything for a couple of weeks. I'll call him as soon as I get back in town and set something up if he's still interested."

"But he wants to talk now. Like, yesterday! Think commission."

Haley did but passed. "I'm in the middle of something here. I can't just drop everything—"

"Since when?"

Haley frowned at the telephone receiver

and Sugar's attempt to be funny. "Sugar, tell me again why I have you as an assistant?"

"Because you love me. You need me, and you know I'll talk straight with you."

Haley could hear the smile in Sugar's voice. She was right on all counts. "Okay, you're right—"

"As always."

Haley rolled her eyes. "Okay, since you are so smart, you figure out what to tell Marcus Sims. I've got my own problems here, so ta-ta for now, girlfriend."

"But—"

Despite the mix of emotions swirling inside of her, Haley hung up the phone. She was going to have to return to her job soon, but it could wait a little longer. She knew now coming home had been the right move for her. Things were shifting into perspective and suddenly she was seeing things in a whole new light. The heaviness she'd carried in her heart about Mule Hollow had lifted for the most part. If the people of the town would have held her back from achieving her goals, they wouldn't have done it intentionally. Listening to them retelling stories about her escapades over Thanksgiving dinner, she'd realized how foolish she'd been harboring hard feelings all these years. They loved her, and thank goodness she was adult enough to see clearly now.

But Will was a different story. A different story altogether. She'd been thinking about what he'd said ever since they'd talked on the playground. Walking to the window of her bedroom, she stared out at the darkened sky and lifted her fingers to her lips. She could almost feel his touch again, soft as a feather. She'd trembled inside when he'd suddenly squatted in front her. His touch had shaken her as deeply as the silken sorrow in his eyes when he'd apologized and melted her heart.

It scared her, actually, this ache that he'd awakened.

In the distance she heard the wailing of a coyote. The high-pitched howl sent shivers down Haley's spine, so lonesome sounding. So desperate.

She turned out the light, climbed into bed and slammed her eyes shut. She had a busy day coming up, and the best thing she could do was to go to sleep now. She was just feeling nostalgic was all. Nothing that rest wouldn't cure. And if that didn't help then a fun day out. Shopping with Lacy and Sheri was bound to cure what ailed her.

At least, as she flopped to her back and felt her bones relax, she was counting on the shopping to cure her crazy head.

After thirty minutes of holding her eyes clamped shut and numerous failed attempts at counting sheep, Haley flopped to her stomach, yanked her pillow over her head and wished for a gun…or a bullhorn. Anything that would send the yowling coyotes deeper into the woods. If she could get rid of them, maybe she could sleep and stop replaying her conversation with Will over and over again in her head.

No such luck. The stinking coyotes refused to leave—and so did thoughts of Will.

Even buried beneath two pillows and her grandmother's quilt, Haley was doomed to spend a sleepless night thinking about the past.

"Hey, what do you think about these?" Sheri Gentry asked as she modeled a set of reindeer antlers. "A red nose and I'm in business, girls," she said, looking like a kid.

Haley picked a red nose out of the bin next to her hip. "Here ya go, Rudolph," she said, tossing it to her. Sheri caught it and held it up near her nose for effect.

They were waiting next to the door, rifling though the different kiddy Christmas display items while Lacy paid for her decorations at the counter.

"Oh, uh-oh!" Sheri squealed, dropping the nose and antlers as she pulled a pair of green elf shoes from the big bin. They were a good ten inches long with upturned toes from which a big red jingle bell swung. Attached to them as a set was a pair of pointed ears that were as big as Haley's hands. "Now this is what I call an outfit! Hey, Lacy, let's buy these." She held them up, nodding enthusiastically. Lacy rolled her eyes, made a face of mock horror, while mouthing an emphatic "No."

Haley chuckled at Sheri's expression of utter dejection.

"You are no fun, Lacy Brown," she grumbled then met Haley's gaze with eyes full of fake annoyance. "I like to call her by her maiden name when I pick on her. Matlock just doesn't sound the same."

Lacy walked over and plopped a bulging bag of candles and ribbons into each of their hands. "Carry those, girls, and let's go get something to eat before we head home. I'm going to work y'all so you're going to need nourishment."

Haley couldn't help liking these two friends. They were like up and down. Lacy was up, and Sheri was down. Lacy served up something funny, and Sheri downed it with flair. Haley had almost called and canceled her date to come shopping with them. She'd awakened feeling as if she'd been plowed over by Applegate's ancient tractor—or the wild hog she'd encountered on her first week in town. However, she'd decided that getting out was probably the best thing she could do for herself. Not only did she want to get to know Sheri and Lacy better, but also she desperately needed a few things to help her make it through the rest of her stay in Mule Hollow.

Not to mention that if she'd stayed home she'd have only thought more about Will. She didn't want to think about him anymore, and she certainly didn't *need* to think about him.

They dropped the bags off at Lacy's car, bantering all the way. Haley was amazed every time she saw Lacy's monstrous pink car. Up until she'd seen the pink 1958 convertible Cadillac sitting in front of Lacy's salon, Haley had only seen the flamboyant make of car in movies or from a distance when an occasional Elvis fan or car buff passed through town. When she'd climbed into it earlier, she felt as if she'd been shot back in time. It was very nostalgic and fun. On the ride to Ranger, Lacy hadn't let the top down because there had been a slight drizzle in the forecast—not, she told Haley, because it was below fifty degrees outside. Cold weather was great fun with the top down, Lacy declared. Haley had a convertible but hadn't tried that one before.

Bags stored safely in the bottomless pit of a trunk, they crossed the street and went to lunch at a new little Italian restaurant that, in Lacy's words, was "to die for."

She was right. Haley loved it. "*Luv*ed it!"

Although normally a lemon cheesecake fanatic, Haley made the mistake of letting them talk her into trying their tiramisu. Big mistake. Haley enjoyed coffee but had never had the coffee-flavored dessert, and she never would again! She got the oversize forkful of creamy dessert in her mouth and couldn't swallow it. It tasted so horrible that her jaws locked, and her throat refused to work. "How," she wanted to know and would have asked out loud if she could have swallowed, "could anyone think *that* was good?"

Much less fabulous? Her eyes started to water and her palms started to sweat by the time she managed to choke it down. Talk about misuse of a good pot of coffee....

All the while Lacy and Sheri laughed, totally insulted that she didn't share their love of the atrocious concoction.

It went without saying that the tiramisu was not the highlight of her day.

The only bright spot in the situation was the double portion of lemon cheesecake she ate to rid herself of the taste.

Later, as they climbed into the car and headed home, they were still teasing her about the horrible facial expressions she'd made. She had to admit she'd probably looked funny.

They continued to have a great time all the way back to Mule Hollow, and when they pulled up in front of the community center, Haley knew she'd made friends for life. She felt relaxed and happy as they unloaded the trunk and clomped into the building intent on getting in some work on the production before the crowd arrived for the evening. Haley had a couple of set designs she wanted to go over with Lacy because she thought she could tweak her drawings a bit and make them better. Following them inside, Haley marveled at how much had been accomplished. But there was still a good bit to be done.

"So, what's up with you and Will?" Sheri asked, cocking an eyebrow. "I just can't hold my curiosity in any longer."

Caught off guard, Haley set her packages down on a table. It wasn't that she hadn't expected questions, but they'd just spent the day together and this was the first time they'd mentioned Will.

Lacy shrugged apologetically. "We know we're being nosy, but we're your friends— at least we want to be. And we wondered if you might need to talk. You don't have to if you don't want to. Say the word and we'll mind our own business."

"Hey," Sheri said, elbowing Lacy. "Speak for yourself. Tell all is my motto. Give us the scoop, girlfriend, because I'm getting some major vibes sparking between the two of you old lovebirds. It's been killing me all day not to ask, but Lacy threatened my life if I didn't make you comfortable first. You're comfortable, right?"

Haley laughed. So they'd planned it all along. She wasn't sure whether to be insulted or relieved that these two cared enough to win her trust first. But, knowing them as she felt she now did, she also knew that they had no agenda except to help and support her. It was something Haley wasn't used to. She'd become so accustomed to being guarded with her thoughts because of the colleagues she worked with that she felt as if God had reached down and given her a gift by placing Lacy and Sheri in her path.

She just didn't know what to say. What could she tell them? She didn't know herself what was going on between herself and Will.

"Well," she sighed, pulling garland and ribbons from the bag because her hands needed something to do. "What can I say? I used to love him."

"Yes!" Lacy whooped, her hand knocking over a candle.

"Whoa, girl," Sheri warned, catching the candle before it hit the ground. "She said *used* to."

Lacy looked sheepish. "Sorry," she squeaked. "I missed that part."

It was easy to do, Haley thought, picturing Will kneeling in front of her as she sat in the swing, his eyes sad....

She ended up telling them about how she'd

felt all those years ago. It was a great relief to talk. In all the years, she'd never told anyone her reasons for running. But Lacy and Sheri listened, consoled and, surprisingly, agreed with her.

"Listen," Lacy said, hugging her. "You did what you had to do. Who truly knows if you messed up or not? What's important is that if you trust God, He can make it all work for good. And if you ask Him, He can lead you in the decisions you make now."

"He helped me," Sheri said, with a wink. "He had His work cut out for Him, but I finally trusted Him enough to see where He was attempting to lead me. So hang in there, and seek Him with all your heart and things will work out. Speaking of my very own heartthrob…" she said.

Haley and Lacy turned to see what she was looking at through the large plate-glass windows. Haley saw Pace sauntering across the street toward the community center, looking as if he'd just stepped off the pages of a Louis L'Amour western.

"That," Sheri sighed, "is the most beautiful man in the world and he's all mine, all mine! God is good. I'll be back to help in a minute."

With that, Sheri hurried out the door and

jogged off the sidewalk to be immediately engulfed in her rugged husband's embrace. Haley's heart sighed at the sight.

"Haley," Lacy said, breaking into her thoughts. "Any time you need to talk, we're here for you. And if you get a wild hair to relocate back here—" she lifted an eyebrow "—you just remember the town can use you."

Haley looked at Lacy. Relocate. There it was again.

Lacy lifted a brow and toyed with a ribbon she'd picked up from the table. "I can't help being an ambassador for Mule Hollow. Your line of expertise would just be a great addition. Mule Hollow is growing and that means the need for houses. What woman is going to want to live in a bunkhouse?"

Haley thought about the colorful town and for the first time really thought seriously about moving home. Could she?

"I don't know, Lacy. That's a big step. I have responsibilities, a great life." The words sounded hollow to her ears; she wondered if Lacy heard it, too.

"But is it the life you want? Just think about it. God has a purpose for everyone, and I'm not saying I know better than you what your purpose is, I'm just saying maybe you could pray about it and be open to options. Being part of building up this town has enriched my life so much. We are building a legacy here that was almost lost until a year ago when the ladies came up with this plan. I really do think you are a link in helping it succeed."

Haley had to admit Lacy made it sound enticing...worthwhile. "Thanks, Lacy. I can't promise anything, but I'll pray about it. Right now I think I'll go make a few changes to the props before the guys get here."

Lacy hugged her. "They look great, by the way. Thanks."

Haley nodded then hurried over to her corner and grabbed a pencil. But before she started to work, she closed her eyes and said a prayer for the Lord to guide her steps.

It felt good to be asking Him for direction and to have friends who supported her in her quest.

Chapter Fifteen

Haley held the nail in place, squinted with one eye and proceeded to let the hammer fall where it would. She was thrilled when it wasn't on her thumb.

"Looks like you got a little better at that than I remember."

Will's soft whisper just beside her made Haley jump, but she didn't squeal and for that she was grateful. When she turned her head to glare playfully at him she almost lost her breath. He was so close, and she knew any sound she'd been tempted to make would have died in her throat.

"I," she said and swallowed hard, her gaze dropping to his lips and the teasing half grin he wore. He looked so much like the college boy she'd fallen for. "I got lucky," she managed to say. He would never know how much the odds had been against her poor thumb making it out of that situation unharmed.

He tugged his hair and stepped back, giving her space. She wondered if he realized that he was making her nervous. Had been all evening.

"Want me to finish it for you?"

"Sure. My thumb thanks you." She handed him the hammer and stood watching as he proceeded to drive the nail home thus making for a much sturdier support behind the painted prop. It was a large rock, one of many that sat out in front of the bridge.

"It takes practice, is all. I've had my share of busted thumbs that had nothing to do with you."

She didn't believe him for a minute, but gave him points for trying to make her feel better about herself. His grin wasn't hurting anything, either.

She laughed. "Yep. They're really fun. I enjoyed myself."

He reached for another nail, his fingers brushing hers as he took it from her open palm. "You seem a little more at ease."

She studied his profile as he hammered in the nail, knowing it was true. At least, it had been, when he met her probing gaze she wasn't so sure how long the feeling would last. The man always had made her knees go weak, and letting her guard down around him made her susceptible to her old habits. Especially the habit of being totally and completely in awe of him. He was a nice man. He'd greeted everyone and offered to help anyone who needed him. The fact that he was helping at all spoke of his generosity. She knew he was pushing himself to meet his deadline, but here he was. Lacy's words were hanging over her shoulder taunting her. *Relocate.* Could she come back to Mule Hollow? Could she take being around Will like this and not find herself lost again?

When his gaze dropped to her lips then lifted to her eyes, she almost jumped back. Despite everything that had happened between them, the chemistry was still there. He felt it, too. It was obvious. Confused, Haley raked her hand through her hair and pulled her eyes away. "I need to go check on the painters," she muttered and hurried away.

She just needed a few moments to get her head back on straight. That was obviously not going to happen standing anywhere near Will.

But even as she picked up a paintbrush to help the other guys paint the river, she knew it would take more than crossing a room to get away from the feelings he'd stirred to life inside of her.

Will wasn't at church on Sunday. Applegate informed Haley, though she hadn't asked for any information, that Will had gone to visit his parents in Austin. Haley was relieved that she didn't have to face him since her thoughts were still befuddled. Her stomach went bottomless every time her mind drifted to Thanksgiving Day beside the swing when he'd admitted that he'd been wrong. And then the way he'd kept looking at her last night as they'd worked together on the props.

The best thing was to stay busy and try not to think about him. She had plenty to keep her busy. With Christmas only four weeks away, Mule Hollow had gone into overdrive decorating the town and gearing up for the Christmas program. Lights were strung down Main Street and boxes of oil lanterns were brought out along with lassos and tinsel. Oh my, was there ever a boatload of tinsel!

She'd had little time to think about much of anything except getting ready for the production. Why, every moment she was being asked to lend a hand with some other project during the day, and the evenings were spent working on props for the play.

She was working on decorating Main Street on Tuesday when Will showed up to install the tracks he'd constructed to make sliding the large backgrounds into place on the stage easier. Haley watched as he and Clint carried the tracks inside. She was busy outside wrapping a porch post in lights and greenery and was glad she hadn't been inside working when he showed up. She couldn't deny that her heart did a rumba knowing he was near. Not trusting her foolish feelings, she intentionally remained outside.

She was standing on a ladder hanging a lantern and paused as her attention was drawn down the street. Applegate and Stanley were supervising the building of a manger scene at the edge of the field where everyone would be parking on the nights of the play. Haley felt sorry for the two bewildered cowboys who were trying to be patient with the checkers players. Single women from miles around loved any excuse they could get to make a trip to the cowboy-laden town, and it was expected that the turnout for this year's Christmas production would be at an all-time high. Haley couldn't help thinking that the two cowboys were enduring a lot to help the cause.

"I feel sorry for Luke and Justin."

At the sound of Will's voice, Haley almost fell off her ladder.

"Steady there," he said, placing his hand on her back. "I didn't mean to startle you."

Haley tried to look unaffected, standing straight on the rung and gripping the roof with her free hand. "Oh, hi. Did y'all get the tracks set?" she asked, hanging the lantern she'd almost dropped. She lost her fight to appear casual and unaffected by his appearance when her boot slipped on the rung as she reached out toward the hook.

Coming to her aid, Will steadied her again with his hand on her back. "Yes, we did. I came to seek your approval." To his credit he didn't say anything about her clumsiness.

"My approval?" she asked, distracted by the feel of his hand casually resting in the center of her back.

"You did do most of the work. I thought it only appropriate that you give the okay."

He held his hand out to her, his eyes twinkling up at her.

He looked so handsome. "I—I'm sure it looks fine," she stammered at the touch of his hand, not wanting to get off the ladder. Not wanting to put her sweaty hand in his.

He frowned. "Haley, let go of the ladder and come look at what we've done. I'm not going to bite, you know."

Challenged, Haley plopped her hand in his just to show him that she wasn't afraid of him. Hoping he would think the heat was making her sweat like a man. She hopped off the ladder and pretended nonchalance. The last thing she wanted was for him to know that he messed with her equilibrium. Pulling her hand free, she strode across the street toward the convention center. "How's your family?" she asked. Oh, yes, that was a good one. Talking about family was a sure sign that she was hunting for solid ground.

"They're good," he said from just behind her. "Mom said to tell you hello, and she said to invite you down for Christmas. Applegate, too."

Haley came to a screeching halt and stared at him. "No. I mean, tell her thank you, but that…well, that would be a little awkward."

Will shrugged. "I told her you would say that. But she said I was to extend the invitation anyway. So that's what I'm doing."

Haley gave him a tight smile. What had she expected—that he would want her to be there?

Inside, she took one look at the track that would help guide the plywood scenes into place and couldn't help smiling openly at him. "That is so cool." It really was. "I thought you guys were going to have to hide behind the curtains and hold the backgrounds in place." Instead, the tracks would hold them up and, like little train-track rail changes, the flick of a lever allowed the backgrounds to interchange with ease. The bridge, which was in three different scenes and quite bulky, would have its own set over to the side and be darkened out when not in use.

"I'm glad you like it."

"I do. This is really going to work well, isn't it?" Hands on hips, she studied the whole setup.

"Believe it or not, yes."

Haley shot Will a sideways glance. "You sound like you had your doubts."

He nodded. "It isn't all about the tracks

working, but everything coming together. When the ladies approached me to help I thought it was a big undertaking. I have so many deadlines to keep straight—my deadline, the Christmas program—it's all running together. I didn't have one hundred percent to give to the production, so if you hadn't been on board there's no way these props would look so fantastic. You saw Nate's Popsicle trees before you enhanced them," he grinned. "That's what we'd be looking at right now if you hadn't used your talents to save the day. Thank you. I think Nate's artwork would have been a distraction from the importance of the story. Not that his help wasn't appreciated."

Haley got the distinct impression that poor Nate would be poked fun at for years for his efforts in the arena of art. "At least he tried," she said.

Will dipped his head to the side. "At least," he echoed and grimaced. His brown eyes danced as they met hers.

"You are going to tease him unmercifully, aren't you?"

He nodded. "Oh, yeah, but not too terribly. It's been a major step to get him involved at all." He paused, his smile gone. "Since his wife died, Nate hasn't done much of anything except work. This has been a step forward for him."

Haley suddenly understood the quiet cowboy more. "I didn't know."

Will shrugged a shoulder. "He's not one to talk about it." He paused, cleared his throat as his gaze touched her gently before he looked away. "He's a good man. This has been good for him. Even if he doesn't believe so."

Haley nodded, moved by the care she heard in Will's voice. She could feel her defenses crumbling.

"Have you eaten?" he asked, catching her off guard.

Haley shook her head before she realized she was setting herself up.

"Then let me buy you lunch?"

Haley bit her lip, told herself she was a grown adult woman and, that being the case, she had nothing to fear from eating lunch with Will.

"That would be nice," she said and immediately saw the folly in her assumption the second he smiled.

Will walked ahead and held the door of Sam's Diner open for Haley, then braced himself for the looks of speculation he knew were coming. He was grateful that Applegate and Stanley were still down the street harassing Luke and Justin. Truth was when Will and Clint had been installing the tracks, Clint pushed him, asking him again what was holding him back from asking Haley out.

There was plenty holding him back. But Will figured lunch was a step forward. Like Nate, this had also been good for Will. Still, it was the only step he was comfortable with and he wasn't too comfortable with that. Although he'd been surprised that Haley said yes to the invitation it was obvious he wasn't the only one uncomfortable.

Will had to give Sam credit when he didn't make a big hoopla of the two of them sitting down across from each other in a vacant booth. Instead, the wiry little man just asked them for their order and went about serving everyone else. Which wasn't many since it was midday and most everyone was out working cattle—except for the two poor cowpokes who'd gotten snared by App and Stanley.

He toyed with the salt shaker as she looked everywhere but at him. "I heard you've been looking at some real estate," Will said, curiosity getting the best of him. Haley looked surprised that he knew.

"I guess I hadn't realized anyone knew I'd been poking around a few places."

He grinned. "Nate saw your car in front of the old Novis place the other day and mentioned it. It's adjacent to his ranch. And Mark Carson saw you over at the Lawsons' abandoned place."

Haley sighed, tilting her head slightly. "I forget, news travels fast out here. Yes, I was just looking. I look wherever I am. I try to gauge the markets."

"Ah, the ladies won't like that. In their minds, they've probably got you halfway moved back."

"They and my grandpa, but it's impossible. I've got too much going on back home. My assistant is driving me crazy. This dead zone and not being able to reach me on my cell has simply done her in. Applegate's answering machine is going to explode if she keeps calling."

"Didn't you have time scheduled for a honeymoon?" He suddenly felt churlish. "Sorry. Tell me to mind my own business if you want."

"I—I had only planned a week. But I…" She paused and studied her hands for a second. "But I really needed a break. I've been running on fumes for months. I didn't know how true that was till I got here. So—" she took a long breath, looking as if it had taken her some time to make the decision "—I'm taking the holidays. If I lose some listings, I just lose them. I need time off."

Will digested that information. "Are you happy, Haley?" He knew he was stepping out where he might not really want to go, but he suddenly wanted to know. He wanted to know if walking away from him had given her everything she'd dreamed of. He wanted to know if walking away from him had been worth it.

"Everyone keeps asking me that. Who's ever happy all the time?" Two lines of concentration stood up between her eyebrows and her lips flattened. "Really, I'm not ecstatically happy. But I'm busy. I like the industry. It's really fast-paced, and the money's ridiculous. Especially compared to this market. The price of homes in California is mind-blowing as a whole. I mean, you have areas out here in Texas, like Austin and some of your other metropolitan areas that are seeing a market boost, but in general, it's crazy on the coast. What?" she asked, pausing.

Will rubbed his jaw. "Nothing," he said. "Listening to you I just realized I've never actually heard you talk about your work. I guess I never thought about you, well—"

She looked straight at him. "You never actually thought about me in a business sense." Her words were flat, her eyes steady.

Will felt their sting of truth. "Yeah," he admitted.

Sam brought their burgers and fries, and told them to enjoy and take their time. He winked at Will before leaving…. So much for Sam not thinking much about Will and Haley sitting together.

"I know it's hard for you to believe, but I'm really good at what I do."

"Haley, I know that."

She lifted her chin slightly. "Really?"

"Yeah, I do. You'd have to be to make it to the level you have. So, what are your plans for the future now that you're not getting married?" The question surprised him. That he wanted to know didn't.

She paused, midbite. "Aren't you full of questions today?"

Will scowled. *Why was he pushing this?*

They were just having lunch. He hadn't planned on giving her the fifth degree. But then he hadn't come to town planning on having lunch with her, either. That had been a spur-of-the-moment decision prompted once more by Clint before he'd gone back to work. Will was going to have a long talk with his friend about minding his own business. At least he and Haley were talking without getting mad at each other. They'd made some progress since she'd first come to town. But, still—

"What about you?" she asked. "Honestly, I don't understand what you did." Her brows crinkled, her expression hardening as she set her food on the plate. "Why would you change all our plans, tell me you'd decided we should live in Mule Hollow, but the minute I left, you left, too."

There was pain in her eyes as she stared him down. He'd started this, but he didn't want to answer her question. He very well couldn't tell her he'd wanted to live in Mule Hollow with her. He couldn't tell her that when she'd left he couldn't take it. Everywhere he'd looked he'd seen her and it had hurt too much. Cut too deep. What was the use? He'd come back after all these years because he'd felt compelled to. It didn't mean that he hadn't thought of her often.

"You left, so what does it matter? You made a choice." He couldn't totally hide the bitterness in his words.

She met his gaze straight on. "Obviously, we both did."

Right after leaving Will at the diner, Haley had gone home and saddled Puddin. Chancing a run-in with another hog suited her mood just fine. She rode the big horse down to the river as her mind replayed their conversation. Will had no idea what she'd done since she'd left him at the altar. He had no idea how lonely her life had been when she'd first run away. She'd gotten a job as a waitress and started going to real-estate school in the evenings…. All the while her heart had been broken. Sure, she'd left three men at the altar. Will kept bringing that up, but he was responsible for her inability to commit. Poor Darin. He'd come into her life when she'd needed a friend. He'd been kind and ambitious and fun, and she'd needed fun and also someone who shared her ambition and respected her for wanting to become something. But she'd never loved him. It had been a whirlwind of a romance in which she'd let her broken heart guide her by trying to forget how Will had hurt her. Darin had fulfilled the gulf that Will hadn't. He'd believed in her ability. They'd planned a quick, cheap wedding…. At least for that one there had only been the two witnesses and the judge to see her run away. She'd come to her senses in time and would have given anything not to have hurt Darin. But she could honestly say that her broken heart had been to blame for what she'd done to him. A person just didn't think rationally when their heart had been betrayed. And that had been Will's fault. Hadn't it?

Staring out across the churning water, Haley fumed. The man truly acted as if he had no idea that he'd done anything wrong. It was baffling. Could he really not get it?

Feeling cold, she rode back through the woods, her mind and heart no more settled than when she'd saddled her horse. It didn't matter because she knew now that she was going back to Beverly Hills as soon as possible. She would make it through Christmas…for Applegate. And then she'd go back to where she belonged. And with any luck she would finally put Will out of her head and her heart.

* * *

Norma Sue had called an emergency meeting of "the Matchmakers of Mule Hollow." Things had stalled between Haley and Will, and the consensus was that they needed to do something quick. They'd thought after the two had shared lunch at Sam's that things would start rolling of their own accord, but instead lunch had killed everything dead in the water. And Applegate, well, he was about to have a conniption. He was trying hard to play it low-key in front of Haley, but the man could just see her slipping from his grasp and leaving him high and dry right after Christmas, if not before. It was all they could do to keep him from marching over to Will Sutton's and giving the cowboy a "kick in the duff," as he called it. Poor Applegate had assumed all he would need to do was put Haley and Will in the same vicinity for a few days, and wondrously the years would fade away, Will would charm her socks off and bam, "Operation: Married by Christmas" would be a done deal.

Not even close.

"So what do y'all think?" Norma Sue asked, looking from Adela to Esther Mae. "Do you think we're going to be able to come through on this for Applegate?"

They were sitting around Adela's kitchen table drinking coffee and eating warm gingerbread.

Esther Mae finished off the big hunk of spicy cake she'd been gobbling down. "That is so delicious. Adela, you have outdone yourself."

Though they had pressing issues to discuss, Norma dropped her chin and gave her friend a warning eyeballing. "You do realize that size twelve you've been so happy about fitting into is disappearing as fast as you're shoveling that cake in?"

Esther Mae dabbed her lips and smiled. "Hush, Norma, I'm allowed a snack. I started on a new diet and exercise program. Hank picked me up one of those miniature trampolines, and I'm jumping on it several times a day now. And having fun, fun, fun!"

Norma grunted, glancing at the bright green velour warm-up suit that Esther Mae wore and the matching headband that fit snugly about her red head. "Like I said, you keep eating that gingerbread like you're doing and that trampoline won't hold up to too much more jumping."

Esther Mae chuckled. "I'm going to tell Hank to pick you up one the next time he's over in Ranger. You could use a little bouncing yourself." She patted Norma's stomach.

"Hey, watch it." Playfully, Norma swatted Esther's hand away. "I made peace with my full figure a long time ago. You're the one always complaining about your weight, so I was just giving you a friendly reminder that tomorrow you're going to regret your indulgence."

Esther Mae plunged her fork into the last piece of gingerbread. "Thank you for caring, but there is no need for you to worry about me. I'm a reformed woman. All I needed to do was add some exercise to my lifestyle. You know, I think I'm going to start walking tomorrow. Now, about Haley Bell, do you think we need to figure out a way to get those two alone together again?"

Adela gingerly set her china cup down then clasped her fine-boned hands together and laid them on the table in front of her. "I've been thinking about that, too. They seem to be getting along fine in the group, but they are avoiding each other. Though their failed lunch date and subsequent avoidance seem to look like a problem, I think that some alone time might be just what is needed."

"I agree," Norma Sue said.

Esther Mae harrumphed. "Well, we need to do it quick. After all, we don't know how long Haley will remain here before going back to the West Coast. So we need to pick up the pace. Christmas is two weeks away and if we want a wedding by Christmas or thereabouts, well something major has got to happen. That's all there is to it."

Norma Sue agreed completely. That was why she'd called the meeting. "That's right. When Applegate asked us to help him bring Haley home, I never dreamed it was going to be so easy to get her back. But I'm getting worried. Real worried. I just figure, like Applegate, that those two were meant for each other. That they just needed to grow up some and things would work out. But I don't know…"

Adela reached for her cup, lifted it to her lips then paused, a thoughtful look in her eyes. "After all these years, you girls know as well as I do that God didn't just happen to bring them both back to Mule Hollow without a reason. It's no accident. We just have to have faith and God will work it out."

"But God didn't just give us this hankering to help them for no reason. So I can't just sit back and do nothing," Esther Mae exclaimed.

Norma chuckled. "Well, then let's get busy and give this covert operation a shot in the leg."

"Oh!" Esther Mae exclaimed and dropped her fork. It clattered on the plate but no one noticed as her eyes lit up and she waved her hands in excitement. "Girls, I've got it. I have the perfect idea!"

Chapter Sixteen

It was ten in the morning and Will found himself standing in front of the community center beside Haley.

Norma Sue smiled at them engagingly while waving a hand-drawn map at him. "So, if you follow these instructions you should have no trouble."

Will took the piece of paper and stared at the drawing wondering how he'd allowed himself to, once again, be roped into doing something he didn't have time for....

But then, he knew how it happened. Norma Sue had told him that Haley had volunteered to go cut the berry branches from some special bush that they just had to have to decorate the tables for the Christmas production. Then she'd told him that Haley might need some help and asked him if he would mind going along just in case.

Of course he would go along. Haley didn't need to be running around out there in the woods alone. Knowing Haley she'd get stuck in a wild hog pen again, and who would be around to find her? Though in an effort of self-preservation, he'd been working hard and trying to avoid her for the last few days, but he couldn't deny that a part of him wanted to go berry picking with Haley.

"Now remember," Norma Sue continued, "they're purple berries."

Haley walked up to where Will and Norma Sue stood in front of the convention center. "Are you certain you want purple berries and not red holly berries?" she asked, stopping just short of three inches from Will's left arm. Will was more than aware that she was standing beside him.

Esther Mae hustled out of the community center just in time to hear Haley's question. "Purple's what we want, Haley. They're just the cutest little clusters of round balls that you'll ever see. And when you see them you'll know exactly why we want them."

Norma Sue nodded. "But if you find some red berries, grab them, too. We can use both colors. Okay, though, y'all better get this show on the road. No sense wasting daylight."

Anticipation skittered through Will and there was no sense denying that it was because he would be spending the next couple of hours with Haley. It was dangerous for his peace of mind, but for right now he didn't care. "Come on, then, you have everything you need?" She tucked her fingers into the pockets of her jeans, rocked forward on the toes of her boots and nodded. He turned to his truck and opened the door of the passenger side for her.

"Are you sure you have time to do this?" she asked, hesitating before she climbed in.

"If I run into trouble getting my deadlines met I might have to teach you how to use a grinder. Are you game?"

She tilted her head back and startled him by smiling up at him, her blond hair sparkling in the morning light like a sunbeam. Looking at her, he knew he didn't care if he had to spend the next week without sleep to get his last two gates finished; the smile on her face was worth it. The next few hours would be his bonus.

"I always did want to learn how to use a grinder."

"Well, y'all have fun out there—oh, hang on a minute, I almost forgot," Norma Sue yelped. Swinging around, she barreled off the steps and yanked open the tailgate of her truck. "Will, come over here and grab this cooler. I put some cold drinks in there and a little snack."

"Exactly how long do you expect us to be out there?" Will asked, looking from Norma Sue to Esther Mae.

"You never know," she said, grinning. "I didn't say purple berries were going to be easy to find."

Knowing exactly what she was doing, he took the cooler and lifted it into the bed of his truck. The ladies never gave up.

"'Bye, now," Esther Mae shouted, waving wildly as he got behind the steering wheel. Haley waved back as he started the motor and then backed out.

He added a quick wave, held back the big grin he was feeling then drove a little quicker than the law allowed down Main Street, toward the deep woods of Clint Matlock's ranch. As they passed Sam's, he thought he saw Applegate's and Stanley's noses plastered to the glass.

"I'm sorry they pulled you away from

work for this," Haley offered, snapping her seat belt in place. "I told them I was more than capable of following the directions and cutting purple berry bushes down. But then they started to fret that I didn't need to be out there all alone. They forget that I grew up running around these woods."

"I don't mind. Besides, someone needs to open the cage doors for you after you run inside."

She smiled and her eyes grew wide. "I hope you didn't tell everyone I got stuck in a hog pen!"

"That's just between us."

"Thank you. Thank you. I could just see it becoming another egg-salad-fiasco story."

Will met her gaze directly. "I'm done with telling stories on you, Haley. I'll just keep that one for myself."

Now why did he go and say that? He focused on the road and tried not to think about the light the statement had brought to her eyes. What did that light mean?

That question tugged at him. "So take a peek at the map and tell me which gate we're supposed to take," he said about five miles down the road. As per the instructions, he turned onto the dirt road that led them deep into what Will classified as some of the most remote untouched land in west Texas. The ladies seriously wanted some berries if they sent them out here.

"Now where?" he asked when they came to a fork in the road. Haley had been quiet. She studied the map Norma Sue had drawn them.

"It says here to take the fork less traveled."

Will shot her a glance. She was staring at him with a question in her eyes. "That's all it says?" he asked.

"Yep."

Tilting his head, he lifted an eyebrow. "You're joking, right?"

Haley mimicked his tilted head with her own then laughed. "Yes, I'm joking. But you looked so serious."

He smiled and suddenly the years seemed to melt away. This was how they used to be together. "So, what does it really say?"

She sighed dramatically, rolling her eyes at him. "It says, take a left at the fork and follow the road to the next cattle guard. Cross it, then follow the fence line down to the creek. Think you can get us that far?"

"I believe I can manage it." He loved the huskiness of her voice and the laughter in her eyes. It was a dangerous thing to acknowledge. But he was feeling dangerous himself.

"I don't know, you'll have to prove it."

Will figured he might have more fun getting them lost. He laughed at the temptation and felt his world grow weightless with the sudden joy of the day.

Looking over at Haley, he knew, dangerous as it was, it was a feeling he could grow used to very easily. He'd been fighting it and trying to deny it. But it was true.

"So, do you see anything?" Haley asked, tugging her coat closer around her. Will was a few feet away from her as they trod through dense woods in search of the infamous purple berry bushes. What kind of bush had purple berries? She was beginning to question their existence. They'd been looking for a couple of hours and had turned up nothing. No berries, at least. Tension between them was escalating with each passing second. Haley was struggling to keep her gaze off Will—which could very well explain the lack of berries. Despite her decision to go back to Beverly Hills, she'd done nothing but think of him ever since they'd shared lunch earlier in the week, and it just wasn't a good thing. It just wasn't. She was beginning to think she was a lost cause.

Will glanced over his shoulder at her, his lips curving at the edges, and her heart thudded like a drum. Feeling unsettled, she stepped forward and tried to focus. "I'm beginning to suspect that there is no purple berry bush," she said and proceeded to step into a pocket of mud. Her boot sank instantly ankle-deep. "Whoops," she gasped, yanking her other foot back before sinking it, too.

"Are you okay?" Will was beside her in an instant, taking her elbow as she tugged her boot free from the muck. It made a nasty slurping sound when it popped free from the suction of the thick goop. But she was only feeling his touch on her elbow.

"That doesn't look so good."

Haley chuckled nervously, holding out the muddy boot. "Brings back memories of when I was a kid roaming around the woods." Moving back a bit, she rubbed the sole of her boot on a thick clump of grass, thinking Will was standing too close, his grin too lethal. "It will be my luck that the only things we're going to find out here are gators and snakes."

"That's what I'm afraid of," Will agreed, his tone serious as his teasing smile disappeared. "The wild hog population and the gator population have grown a lot since we were kids. It's getting to be a major problem."

They were walking again but Will stopped suddenly, put his hands on his hips and surveyed the area, his expression grim. "Come on, we're going back to the truck. I don't want you to get hurt, and it's getting colder anyway."

Haley scowled. "You're joking, right?"

He shook his head. "No. I'm not."

"Will, I'm not going to freeze. And the ladies wouldn't send us out where there were alligators. Even if there were any out here, you know as well as I do that those animals are as afraid of us as we are of them. Besides, we can't go back empty-handed. What would we say—"Sorry, we got cold'?"

Haley had enjoyed the morning very much and she didn't want to admit it to Will, but frankly, she wasn't ready to go back yet. Not because of gators or snakes, but because going back would mean her time with Will would be over. They were getting along as if she'd never run away from Mule Hollow. It was as if they'd both left their past at the crossroads where the dirt road met the pavement. And though she might be flirting with a broken heart again, she hadn't had this much fun in years.

"I used to love to wander around out in the woods at Applegate's. I hadn't realized until the other day when I took the horse out how much I'd missed country life."

Reaching out, she grabbed Will's hand and tugged him up the embankment away from the stream. "Come on. If there's a purple berry out here then we are going to find it. So buck up, buddy, and put those eyes to work."

He groaned. "I forgot how tenacious you could be."

When they reached higher ground, all too aware of the feel of his fingers clasped tightly around hers, Haley let go of his hand. She'd grabbed it impulsively, and it was the last thing she needed to be holding. Shaken by his touch, she missed seeing the log in her path, stumbled over it and plunged forward, headfirst down another hill.

She barely had time to scream before she hit the ground, rolled a few times then landed flat on her back in the middle of a bank of cold, wet mud beside the stream.

Dazed and aching, Haley lifted her head and the only good thing she saw about landing in the frosty, mushy mud was that at least she hadn't landed on top of the alligator lounging contentedly three feet away from her.

Her brain repeated the information with a bit more urgency. *Alligator!*

But her response was to continue to stare at the prehistoric-looking creature with its flat rounded snout and beady eyes. It was as startled to see her as she was to see it. Still, her fear won out when it lifted out of the mud on its ugly squat legs and hissed at her like a mad cat on steroids.

Okay, so at least if she *had* landed on top of the thing she might have been lucky enough to knock it unconscious instead of being its lunch. Which apparently she was about to become.

She'd been too busy tumbling down the hillside and meeting up with the six-foot-long gator to realize that Will had tripped on the same log and was tumbling down the hill right behind her. That was, until all one hundred and eighty-five pounds of him landed facefirst in the mud between her and the hissing gator.

It all happened in a matter of seconds, and it was over quicker than that. Thanks to the good Lord, Mr. Gator, aka Chicken Little, took one look at Will's sludge-covered face as Will lifted up from the mud and took off! Haley watched in shocked amazement as the scaly beast trotted away, tail swaying in its wake.

Will's face was so slimy with mud that Haley didn't blame the reptile. But she was so relieved to see the gator's tail disappearing into the stream ten feet away that instead of screaming or running, she sat up and did the unthinkable—she laughed.

Not a good thing to do in the presence of an angry man.

"What are you laughing at?" Will yelled, scrambling out of the mud watching the water ripple where the small gator had just disappeared. Will was shaken by how close Haley had just come to being attacked by the animal. Reaching down, he grabbed her by the arms and hauled her up out of the mud to hold her close. He'd been so intent up on the hill watching her eyes dance that he hadn't seen the log. When she'd flown forward, he'd lunged for her, hit the same obstruction, and followed her straight down the hill—and into the path of the alligator. Thank goodness God had put him between her and the gator.

"Are you all right?" he asked now, angered at his carelessness. Alarmed at the thought of what had almost happened to her, he pulled away and ran his hands quickly down her arms then back up to her shoulders. They were both covered in mud, but he didn't care. He had to make sure she hadn't broken anything—had to make certain she was safe.

"I'm fine, Will. Really, God was just having a good laugh at us today is all. What are the odds?" She looked shaken despite her words.

"That's it. No more discussion. We're getting out of here." Taking her hand, he started to lead her back up the hill, but she held back.

"Will, stop!" she exclaimed, pulling her hand out of his grasp.

He spun around at her exclamation. "What?" he yelled, scanning the area, arms outstretched and ready for a fight, expecting the alligator to be charging them.

"Purple berries, there," she sang like a kid spying cookies. Sidestepping him, she slogged through the six inches of mud to the far hill where a grouping of thin scraggly limbed bushes covered with clusters of purple berries dotted the terrain.

"*Haley,* enough already. Forget the berries. You're covered in mud and it's getting colder, not to mention there could be another alligator in there. Now come on."

Haley ignored him as she marched right up the hill to the first bush and fingered the ugly clump of purple berries. They looked like red holly berries but were bright purple, and though Will had seen them before he had no idea what their name was nor did he give a hoot. What he cared about was getting Haley safely home before she caught a cold or got her arm bitten off. Something she was completely oblivious to considering. He'd always had to look out for her and now was no different.

"You just wait until I get back to town," he growled. "Norma Sue should never have asked you to come out here."

Haley turned toward him. Mud was clinging to one side of her cheek; her hair was wet on one side and her skin was pink with chill. But her eyes were on fire as she pinned them on him, startling him with her intensity.

"You will do no such thing, Will Sutton.

Norma Sue asked me to find the berries. She didn't force me or know she was putting me in danger. The odds of me running into an alligator or falling over a log are low. It is not her fault that today was not my day." She proceeded to reach into the pocket of her coat and pull out the canvas laundry tote Will had watched her carefully fold and place there earlier.

Frustrated, he scrubbed mud off his chin and realized he'd lost his hat in the fall. Deciding he would be better served by calming down, he spun and stalked back across the mud in search of his hat. He spotted it up the hill by the log that had caused this whole fiasco. Stomping toward it, he wondered why he was so upset. It wasn't as if he hadn't grown used to the unexpected happening when Haley Bell was around. That was part of her being her. She attracted, or caused, no one knew what it was for sure, the unexpected. Growing up, she'd always been the little kid that weird things happened to. Sweet little Haley Bell. Everyone had loved her, and loved to tease her, but one day when he'd come home from college he'd realized she wasn't little Haley Bell anymore. That summer he'd fallen in love with the woman she'd become, and part of that love included an overwhelming desire to protect her. Many times that included protecting her from herself.

A hard thing to do when she was always running ahead of him, like tripping over the log before he could get a grasp on her. How did a man protect someone who wouldn't slow down and try to protect herself? Especially a woman who knew that trouble and mishap preceded her?

Will snatched up his hat, wincing when a strained back muscle protested the maneuver. It was a wonder they hadn't broken their necks careening down that hill.

He didn't put the hat on, not wanting to transfer the mud in his hair to the inside of the Stetson. Instead he took the time to reshape it, fighting for calm, then he hung it from a tree limb and marched back toward Haley.

She was happily snapping berry stems from the bush and dropping them into the bag, totally oblivious to the fact that he was in crisis. The woman had been controlling him since he'd been a sophomore in college with this overwhelming need to protect her. He wanted to march down there, grab her and carry her back to town whether she was ready or not. But what he wanted to do more than anything else was hold her and kiss some sense into her.

Or just kiss her.

He'd lost more than his pride when he'd rolled down that hill like Jack after Jill. He'd obviously lost his head…and any brains he'd once had there.

Chapter Seventeen

Haley was well aware that she was making Will mad. But it was better for him to be mad at her; it protected her from herself in a way. And right now she needed protection because she wasn't thinking straight.

Crazy her—she wanted to kiss Will Sutton.

Mud and all, it didn't matter that they were both gooey messes. She wanted what she wanted and that was to feel his arms around her and his lips pressed against hers in a long precious kiss. She'd felt so loved when he'd held her. Always had. *Haley, what are you thinking?*

She snapped the berry-laden twigs as if it were their fault she was such an irrational human being.

Glancing over her shoulder, she saw Will stalking toward her. He'd wiped most of the mud from his face, but he hadn't put his hat on and no wonder. His hair had started to stiffen with mud as if he'd prettied it up with hair gel. But one look in his eyes assured her that Will Sutton wasn't feeling like a pretty boy. He was hot, hopping mad and it showed with every stiff step he took.

Haley geared up for battle. If he thought all he had to do was crook his finger and she'd jump like when they were young, he was wrong.

Dead wrong.

She'd been flirting with this attraction and now knew she'd dived right back into being a fool. Yup, big stupid, glossy-eyed fool. "Don't start, Will," she snapped. "I'm going to fill this bag up with these berry branches, so just back off. Shoo, go sit over there," she said, waving a hand toward where his hat hung on a tree limb. "If you think I'm the little girl who used to follow you around like a little lamb, well, you're wrong. I might have had a moment—" She stopped herself before she goofed by admitting she'd been thinking about kissing him. "I mean, well—" she threw her shoulders back so hard she almost threw her back out "—I'm a grown adult who can pick berries and face alligators if I want. You can't control my life—"

She was startled when Will didn't even pause as he reached her. One moment she was laying down the law to him, and the next she was in his arms and he was kissing her.

Huh—Haley's arms dropped to her sides. The bag of berries, forgotten, thudded to the ground at their feet.

She'd always loved Will's strength. His ability to make her feel safe—that was until he tried to take over. But since she had been daydreaming about his kiss and being held in his arms, for this moment she let her defenses slide away as easily as she'd dropped the purple berries. Her hands came around him, felt the power of his muscles through the light layers of his jacket, and she gave in to the wonderful sensation of his lips on hers.

Haley knew she was in dangerous territory. Had been slowly moving toward it all morning, as her emotions had waffled between what had been and what could have been. Somewhere overhead a bird shouted out its glee at being allowed to soar high above the world, and Haley lifted her hand to cup Will's jaw, soaring in her own blue sky.

Will drew back and their gazes locked. His eyes were searching just as she knew hers were. All these years…the thought, the memory of how she'd loved him, overwhelmed her and she closed her eyes, swayed toward him and felt his arms tighten around her again. He whispered her name against her lips then kissed her again.

There was nothing tentative about Will's kiss. He always had put his heart and soul into kissing her. It was one of the things that she'd never been able to forget…and no one had ever matched the feelings that kissing Will always evoked inside of her. His kisses were connected to her heart.

And nothing had changed.

The world seemed to spin around them, as the kiss went on and on. When at last they parted, Will rested his forehead against hers, continuing to hold her close as if he never wanted to let her go. Haley's world had turned on its side, and she wasn't sure she would be able to stand if he let her go.

They were in the shadow of the woods; filtered sunlight sprinkled across the ground at their feet. Haley studied those feet while she struggled to get her bearings. Will's boot, her boot, Will's boot, her boot…alternated, intertwined like the pairing of a man and woman. It was about the most perfect picture Haley had ever seen.

It was as if they were woven together, as one, just the way the Lord had intended. That she'd longed for the love she'd hoped they'd shared. The love that had been nothing but smoke in the end. As if she'd just had a bucket of ice water thrown in her face, Haley suddenly jumped back. "Whoa!" she exclaimed. What was she doing?

What was she thinking? This could never work.

Never!

No. Not just never.

But never, *ever!*

Grabbing the bag of berries, blinded by fury and frustrations, Haley stormed up the hill and down the other side. She adjusted the bag on her back and stepped over the log, heading in the direction of the truck.

There she went again, jumping into the middle of something without a plan. Kissing—yes, *kissing*—Will Sutton was not a plan. It had been tempting. There was no doubt about that. The very idea had been floating around in her head from the moment she'd rolled her window down a few short weeks ago and found him looking down at her—but it was not a plan.

The man confused her. The man infuriated her. The man made her heart stop and her pulse race, but that in itself was not a plan. He'd hurt her. He'd let her down. It was not anything except crazy.

Capital letters CRAZY!

"Haley, would you wait up?" Will demanded.

He'd caught up with her and was standing right behind her, and the knowledge caused her insides to tremble. But she was done with that. Spinning around to tell him so, she almost collided with him in her haste.

Why was it the man, even caked in mud, could turn her world upside down? It wasn't fair.

What, she wanted to know, was fair about that?

What was fair about a woman loving a man who…? "Look, Will, this, this whatever it is would never work. That kiss should never have happened. Years ago you fell in love with a goofy girl who could barely think for herself. Believe me, I know!" Haley's hands tightened around the tote, her clutch mimicking the band that was tightening around her heart. "And when I finally did start to think, you couldn't accept it. You didn't believe I could ever make anything of myself." That thought hurt then and it hurt even more now.

He shook his head, his eyes wide. "That isn't true. Do we always have to come back to this? Come on, Haley." He stepped near her, his voice softening. "We had something. I've realized I messed it up. But I want to start over. Believe me, I've tried to talk myself out of it—"

"Tried to talk yourself out of it?" Haley gasped, the band around her heart so tight she thought she was going to scream. Instead, she spun and slogged through bushes. She was so mad at herself and at him. She would have relished a fight with a stinking gator. She'd told him before when he'd tried to apologize that it was okay, but it wasn't. Not when he couldn't acknowledge what it was that he'd done. "You tried to talk yourself out of admitting that you let me dow—" She stopped herself, stomped her foot and glared back at him. "Yes! We do have to keep going back to this. I thought we didn't, but I was delusional. Because I've suddenly realized something. Something important. Something so very important—you never loved me." She tossed the fact over her shoulder and kept on walking.

Until Will snagged her by the arm, bringing her to a halt as scalding tears brimmed at the backs of her eyes and threatened to humiliate her. "Haley," he breathed, gently tugging her around. "I did love you. If you'd have bothered hanging around long enough for our wedding, I'd have been proving my love to you every day since."

Haley yanked her arm out of his grasp, the lie breaking her. "Get away from me. Get as far away from me as you can get, because if you so much as look at me sideways I'm going to—"

Will dropped his hands and stared at her as if maybe he didn't know her as she yanked open the truck door and climbed inside.

She couldn't blame him. She didn't know herself, either, right now.

They didn't speak all the way back to town. Haley looked straight ahead. She was so mad, so unbelievably angry, that she couldn't think. Much less think straight. She tried. She tried to make her mind work, but it wouldn't happen. Her brain just kept clicking back to furious.

Clicking back to the pain.

The pain she'd tried so hard to keep away. So hard to cover up. So very hard to forget. But it was useless and she knew it.

Will Sutton had let her down in the worst way. She had loved him so much. She could not, would not, let herself fall prey to that kind of hurt again. That kind of hurt made her weak. And she refused ever to be that weak again.

Haley was not any happier by the time they pulled into town a few minutes later and she realized that she was going to have an audience watching her as she stepped out of the truck.

Perfect. Just perfect. She was covered in mud and fuming, but she didn't care. Really, it was liberating, actually. This would be the Haley Bell story to last a lifetime and she didn't care.

Why, goodness, it was her Christmas present to the town. Perfect.

Will slammed the truck to a halt in front of the center. As if they'd all been staring out the windows waiting on them to appear down the lane, the sidewalk was packed before she could slouch out of the truck cab.

"Haley Bell, what happened to you?" Esther Mae exclaimed, and she was echoed by Norma Sue and several others.

Haley could only imagine how she must look with her hair plastered in mud-hardened ribbons to her scalp, her clothes stiff with mud. She snapped, crackled and popped with each step as she stalked to the bed of the truck and yanked the half-filled bag of purple berries out of the bed. Slamming the bag over her shoulder, she finally spoke. "*He* happened," she said, glaring at Will, who'd also limped stiffly to the back of the truck. She ignored the exasperation she saw in his eyes, hiked her nose in the air and walked to the sidewalk. She knew she was acting crazy, but she couldn't stop herself. Feelings were warring inside her that she couldn't face.

Lacy and Sheri came skidding to a halt by the door.

"Haley," Lacy gasped.

Applegate stepped out of the crowd, his bony chest bowed out and fight in his eyes. "What did he do? Come on, tell us."

"He, he," Haley sputtered, faltering with

why exactly she was acting like this. "He *kissed* me. That's what he did!" She glared at Will, and he glared back.

"Kissed you," Applegate said, his face drooping into a frown as he scratched his head and looked from her to Will, then over to Norma Sue, Esther Mae and Adela, who were standing in a huddle looking stunned.

"Did she say he kissed her?" Stanley barked, stepping around Applegate and fiddling with his hearing aid.

"Yes," Haley snapped again, her ire rising as smiles blossomed across everyone's faces.

"That's what I thought she said," Stanley mumbled, looking dumbfounded. "Ain't that what was s'posed to happen?"

Haley groaned, dropped the bag of berries, threw up her hands and stormed into the building, intent on getting as far away from Will as she could get.

No such luck. He stomped in behind her, hands on hips, his brown eyes flashing like molten honey when she glared at him.

"You kissed her?" Esther Mae squealed as everyone filed in behind him.

"Yeah, I kissed her," Will growled.

"Well, Will," Norma Sue managed to say,

suppressing laughter. "Whatever in the world would make you go and do something terrible like that?"

Chuckles rippled through the crowd of people. Haley glared at Lacy and Sheri, who immediately coughed back their laughter and tried to look serious as Esther Mae bumped them out of her way and wiggled farther into the room. She was grinning as bright as a neon sign on a cloudless night.

Will just stood there glaring at Haley, and she glared right back at him.

"Will!" Applegate snapped. Haley realized he was about as happy behind his scowl as a frog in a bug-infested lily pond. "What do ya have to say fer yourself?"

"I think when I rolled down that hill and landed beside that gator I must have hit my head hard," he answered, his voice low and barely controlled. Then with a last shake of his head, he spun on his heel and stalked out the door, got into his truck and was gone.

"Did he say *gator?*" Stanley asked, breaking the silence as all eyes turned to Haley.

Chapter Eighteen

"What'd ya do to my Haley Bell?" Applegate demanded, glaring though Will's screen door. Will had been expecting him ever since the disaster of yesterday. He still didn't understand what had happened. But every time he thought about it, he got madder. There had been no talking to the woman. None. He'd spent a sleepless night tossing and turning, and seeing her face and how incensed she'd been.

And all because of a kiss.

Well, not just any kiss.

A weak-kneed, melt-his-bones kiss that had set his world on end.

Will forced the thoughts away and stared at Stanley, who was bowed up worse than Applegate, his plump face all knotted with the desire to wring Will's neck:

Disgusted with the whole situation, Will pushed the screen open. "Come on in and let's get this over with." He stalked down the hallway toward his kitchen. "Might as well face this over coffee."

Grabbing three mugs, he set them on the table then poured the steaming coffee into them, motioning for App and Stanley to sit. Will opted to lean against the counter and take what they had to say standing. A man didn't take a woman out and bring her back covered in mud, madder than the dickens, and not expect trouble. Will had known better than to kiss her. He'd known it in his gut. He'd done it anyway, and now he had to face the consequences.

"Will." Applegate opted to stand, too, as he belted his question out loud enough to disturb the cows in the pasture. "What do ya have to say fer yerself? I didn't work so hard ta git my Haley Bell home for you to run her off afore we married her off."

Will glowered at Applegate standing tall and as rigid as the $1.98 stiff-starched, button-down shirt he wore. "Run her off?"

"Yup," Stanley answered, his lips flattening into a hard line. Anger didn't look right on the usually affable man. "She done started packing. Applegate had ta sneak outside and diddle with her car so's she couldn't drive off like she'd told him she was going ta do first thang this morning."

Will had known he'd upset Haley with the kissing. It had blown him away and, sure, he shouldn't have crossed that line, but he'd thought they might talk about it after she'd calmed down. He'd thought he'd have time to at least reason with her and try and make sense out of everything she'd said. He hadn't thought she'd run off. Then again, wasn't that what she did? She always ran.

He was so tense that his entire body ached with frustration. Angry, he turned away and slammed his palms into the kitchen counter. Leaning his weight on his arms, he willed himself to think straight.

What did God expect from him?

He was no saint. He raked his hand down his face.

"Don't worry, son, I stopped her for now. 'At little piece of metal she calls a car ain't going anywhere fer the time being. And I done stopped by Purdy's mechanic shop and told him that if she calls him ta come take a look at her car that he ain't s'posed to go out to my place under any circumstances."

"So what do you want me to do? If she wants to leave, then who am I to stop her?" Will turned and leaned against the counter.

Applegate and Stanley were both staring at him as if he were the dumbest cowpoke on the block.

"Don't you think it's about time you and that little gal of mine worked out yor differences? I mean really, son, I got her here. I can't do every thang for you. And I kin tell ya that sitting around here in your house ain't gonna fix nothing."

Will studied his bare feet and decided now wouldn't be the best time to point out to them that it was six-thirty in the morning and barely light outside.

The fact that he'd hardly slept at all didn't mean much, but he'd been debating his situation all night. "App, I won't lie to you. I've still got feelings for Haley. But there are just some things that aren't meant to be. The woman hates me."

Stanley looked from Will to Applegate and back to Will. "Who told you that bunch of hogwash? For a smart fella, you ain't so smart. Here's the deal. Me and Applegate and all the ladies are gonna do our best at keeping that little gal from taking flight

again. And if you don't figure out how to
hold her, it's gonna be everybody's loss when
she leaves. But mostly yours. Come on App.
We done all we kin do here."

Will watched Stanley storm down the hall
and slam through the screen door. Applegate
was as stunned as Will and didn't make a
move at first. Finally, he shook his head, then
followed his buddy.

"She's at my house. Now get yor shoes on
and get out there."

Will figured it was pretty bad when a man
had a couple of old codgers telling him how
to run his love life.

Not that he had a love life, he thought
glumly.

Haley's first reaction to his kiss had been
inspiring. For a brief moment his world had
been right and he'd felt the sun come out. For
a moment it was as if the Lord was smiling
on him, and then like a light switch clicking
off she'd pulled out of his arms and marched
up that hill.

Needless to say, it hadn't been his best
moment.

What had he done that was so unfor-
givable? All these years he'd blamed her. But
Haley, his sweet, gullible Haley had run

because in her opinion, he'd let her down. She'd denied it Thanksgiving Day, denied that he'd cut her so deep. But it was more than apparent that what he'd done to her went far deeper than she was letting on.

Though he wanted to say she was all wrong… he couldn't. Not totally. He hadn't given her the chance to spread her wings. Instead he'd chosen to try and protect her from a harsh world outside the county line surrounding Mule Hollow. In doing so he'd asked her to choose between his love and her dreams.

He'd given her no choice. What would she have been if he'd held her back?

Will took a long hard look at himself and didn't like what he saw.

But he knew the truth now. He'd sent Haley running, and it was up to him to get her to stop. No matter what it cost him.

Will waited until nine o'clock to drive over to Applegate's place. There wasn't any sense making her angrier in case she'd decided to sleep late… although the boys had assured him she was planning on rising early to hit the road. That being the case, he wanted to give her a little time to adjust to the fact that she was stuck.

He pulled up the drive and parked his truck beside Haley's car. Pausing as he closed the truck's door, he glanced around the yard. The wind had picked up and the sting of it whispered that the temperature was dropping yet again. Flipping his collar up, Will strode onto the porch and knocked on the heavy wooden door.

After the second knock, he went in search of Haley. Thinking she may have gone for a ride, he walked toward the barn to check things out. Applegate's house was an older place, a sprawling ranch of brick and wood, and his barn was a classic—red plank two-story. There was a hayloft up top and stalls below that lined both sides of a wide alley.

The double doors were slightly open. Inside, the barn smelled of sweet hay and horses. Walking down the center alley between horse stalls, it only took one look to see that Haley hadn't taken any of them out for a ride, so she had to be somewhere nearby.

"Hey, Puddin," he said when the curious horse stuck her head over the gate. "Where's our girl?" Will asked, reaching out to rub the star between her eyes before turning to head back out the way he'd come. He was midway down the alley when he heard a sound and looked up—just in time for a huge pile of loose hay to land on his head. He barely had time to duck his chin before it covered him.

"I'm not your girl," Haley snapped.

So much for her having calmed down, Will thought, shaking off the hay and looking up at her. She stood with pitchfork in hand, beat-up cowboy hat, jeans stuffed into her boots and watched him with cool eyes.

"Real funny," he said, pushing his hat up with his thumb.

"It wasn't meant to be."

She sounded about as friendly as the hissing alligator had the day before. But she was dazzling standing up there looking like Elly May Clampett, and Will couldn't stop the smile that spread across his face.

Haley's brows met and her lips flattened. "Will, go home, please."

She sounded sad, and all he wanted was to make her smile. To let her know that he knew she was struggling. "I can't. Not until you come down here. We need to talk."

Her eyes clouded and her grip tightened on the pitchfork.

"But leave the pitchfork up there, please. I'd feel safer." He watched her as she shifted her weight from one leg to the other. Then, just when he thought she might tell him to get lost, she jammed the pitchfork into the hay bale and climbed down the ladder.

"So," she said, crossing her arms and pinning him with wary eyes. "I'm listening."

"I heard you were leaving."

"Applegate tell you that?"

Will nodded, and she rolled her eyes.

"I should have known. I told him I was leaving as soon as I woke this morning. But, now I think I'm being held prisoner," she huffed.

Despite the emotions rippling inside of him, Will had to fight a smile…. This was his Haley Bell. A bit of fire and sweet all wrapped up together. "What makes you say that?" he asked just because he wanted to hear her explain it.

"My car won't start, and no one will come out and take a look at it. Purdy went fishing." She looked disgusted. "Like I believe that. And everyone else had *pressing* business that had to be tended to today, so no one else, all five that I called anyway, could get over here today, much less this morning, to help me."

Will took his hat off, held its rim with both hands and studied it for a long moment. "If you'll hear me out, then I'll see what I can do about it."

She studied him for a long moment; Will could see her mind working. And he prayed he didn't say something stupid. He'd finally started thinking after Applegate and Stanley left this morning. He'd also spent some quality time with the Lord praying for direction. He'd realized that God might have given him a second chance, but if he were to ever have a future with Haley, then they needed time. He needed her to stick around.

"Look, Haley. I let you down in the worst way. I know that now, but that doesn't mean I didn't love you. It just means I was a blind fool."

Her expression was uncompromising as she stared at him, green eyes as bright as emeralds in sunlight, her jaw set at an unforgiving slant. The woman could be as stubborn as a mule sometimes. Shifting from boot to boot, Will slapped his hat against his hip then rammed a hand through his hair. He'd just basically said he loved her, and she acted like she hadn't even heard him. He knew there was more to this than she was acknowledging; he'd felt it in the way she'd responded to his kiss. A woman couldn't hide something like that. It was what gave him hope that with time he could right this wrong. But this wasn't about him, at least not for the immediate time being. This was about Haley and Applegate, so he backed away from his feelings and focused on what he'd come to do.

And that was to right another wrong he'd caused.

Feeling as jittery as if she was about to jump from an airplane without a parachute, Haley took a step away from Will. Even though she was still mad at him, she couldn't deny that he fuddled her brain when he was so close. Now that a little time had cooled her temper, the irrational part of her was starting to think about how wonderful she'd felt for those brief moments that she'd been in his arms. Distance wasn't helping as she took a steadying breath, hoping to clear her head. But nothing was helping because he'd said he'd loved her. Back then, all those years ago.

But she summoned up some outrage at the irony that he sure had a funny way of showing that love. What did that say about a man when he was so caught up in himself that he had no concept of how he'd hurt her by his lack of belief in her? The scars of his betrayal had impacted everything she'd done from that moment on.

Though she was physically and emotionally attracted to him even now, that deep anger that had erupted from her when he'd kissed her still left her shaken. She'd never known so much rage and resentment lived inside of her. His kiss had brought it all up, and she'd cracked under the pressure. The fact that he looked so contrite and concerned irritated her more.

"What do you want, Will?" she said tersely, just wanting him to leave. The man had no concept of loving her for who she really was. From his actions back then he'd proved that he loved the idea of her only as the balm that boosted his ego, that he adored the package as long as the brain stayed dormant and out of his way. That he would make the decisions that would determine their life and toss her needs to the side. That wasn't love. Not the kind of love she ever wanted a part of. No matter what, she wouldn't let herself weaken enough to go there again.

"Look, I stepped out of line yesterday and

I'm sorry. We have a past together. A history that we will always share. And I have to admit that the selfish part of me wants to keep you here so that I can convince you to give us another chance. But, Haley, here's the deal. If you were to leave here again because of me and deprive Applegate of the holidays with you, I'd never forgive myself. So I'm asking you, whether you forgive me or not, I'm asking you to stay until Christmas, at least, for Applegate. This isn't about us, but about you and your grandfather. Please stay. I'll stay away from you if that's what you want. I promise. I'll keep out of your way as much as humanly possible. And I won't say another word about my feelings."

Haley knew he was telling the truth where Applegate was concerned. "I'll think about staying until Christmas," she said. "But no trying to kiss me. I can't think straight when you kiss me." She shouldn't have said that and wasn't happy that she'd admitted it to him.

He held her gaze steady, locked his jaw hard, and she got the distinct feeling that he, like she, was remembering the kisses they'd shared the day before.

"I said I'd stay out of your way. That means no more kisses," he said at last. "If that's what it takes for you to stay around for a little while. Applegate deserves that, Haley. And I'm sorry that I got in the way of it. I'll go now. I just thought you needed to know how I felt." He started to leave, then paused as if to add something but instead spun away and left her to think.

Applegate did deserve more from her. She'd already acknowledged it, and here she was about to run again. He'd been there for her every step of her life, and what had she done for him?

Will was striding purposefully away from her. She followed at a slower pace. At the barn door, she watched him get into his truck, feeling a tug of tears for lost dreams. When he turned to give her one last look, she lifted her chin almost as a shield against the emotions she saw written in his expression. She wasn't sure what she saw there.... Anger, sadness, regret...love?

Regret. She knew that one well, so welcome to the club. Because of him, she felt as if her entire life had been one long regret after the other. And this disastrous *thing* between them was the root of it. A blast of ice-cold wind swept around the corner of the barn and hit Haley full force, stinging her cheeks and making her eyes water. She gasped and told herself the tears slipping from her eyes were simply a reaction to the bite of the air. But watching him leave caused her heart to swell, as if it would burst. She swiped at her eyes with the back of her hand. Will Sutton had ruled her life from the moment she'd first fallen in love with him.

It was true. Every turn, good or bad, she'd ever made had been because of her love for him or her anger at him. She'd said she didn't look back, but everything behind her had driven her to become the woman she was today. Even now, she was making choices for her future based not on what she wanted but on what she was trying to leave behind. And that was Will. To be honest, in the beginning it had been the town not letting her grow up, but it was mostly Will that fueled her choices now.

It wasn't right. She'd been exhausted and on the verge of depression when she'd arrived here weeks ago. She closed her eyes and threw back her head in frustration as more tears threatened.

She had to get off the merry-go-round.

She had to break the cycle.

It was so simple. What did she want? What

did she want to do with her life? What would make her happy?

She didn't exactly have answers, but she did know running back to Beverly Hills wasn't the answer.

Haley sucked in the frigid air, then hurried across the yard and up the steps into her grandpa's house.

The last thing he'd urged her to do before she went to sleep the night before was to ask God to guide her. She'd been too upset and angry to turn to God. Not only now, but for years. Yet, she felt an overwhelming need to talk to Him now. She could blame Will for only so much. She was an adult and if she ever wanted to respect herself, she had to be accountable for her own choices.

Sinking into a chair at the table, Haley let her gaze roam slowly around her grandparents' home. "Dear Lord." The words came out cracked and awkward. Her eyes rested on the picture of her grandparents on the hall wall. Their smiles urged her to continue.

It was time to change her life. She might not understand what was going to make her happy, but she finally understood that to figure it out and be happy, really happy…she had to confront her problems straightforwardly and not by looking back.

She bowed her head and started over. "Dear Lord." Her words were stronger, fueled by conviction. If she wanted change in her life, then she had to mean it and it had to start with sincere prayer.

Chapter Nineteen

"Thanks for the lift, Lacy," Haley said, hopping out of the Caddy.

"You call me anytime. And, Haley, I do believe God has a plan for you here."

Haley glanced toward the diner then back to Lacy. "I'm not sure what He has planned for me. But I think that if Applegate wants me to hang around here badly enough to sabotage my car, and I really do think he did—" she smiled at his antics, both funny, yet sad, to her "—then I'm going to do it."

"But are you happy? Haley, you've got to be happy."

"Lacy, it's been so long since I was truly happy that I'm not sure what that is anymore. But I feel confident that this is the right thing to do. Do you know what I mean?"

Lacy smiled, reached a hand out and laid it over Haley's resting on the car door. "I do. I'm praying for you. And I hope you know that Jesus says to approach the throne of grace with confidence, so that we may receive mercy and find grace to help us in our time of need. Haley, you have a lot going on. Please remember that God will help you."

Feeling confident that turning to the Lord had been the first right decision she'd made in a long time, Haley squeezed Lacy's hand. "Thank you. Okay, time to break the news. See you later."

Taking a deep breath, she spun and walked up onto the sidewalk and through the swinging doors into the diner.

The jukebox was just finishing up a lively Jerry Lee tune with the man burning up the piano keys as she entered. Instantly, greetings rushed in to fill the ensuing silence.

It was, she realized, not something she'd ever get living anywhere but Mule Hollow.

"Hello, Haley Bell."

"How's it going, Haley Bell?"

"Looking good today, Haley Bell!"

Feeling more sure about her decision, she waved at each person and moved to the windowseat where Applegate and Stanley were bent over an intense game of checkers. Suspiciously intense, as a matter of fact. So much so that they hadn't heard all the commotion she'd stirred up walking in—yeah, right. She knew from where they were sitting that they'd seen her get out of Lacy's car. It was more than apparent to her that they were pretending because they obviously had something to hide. Like incapacitating her car.

She placed her hands on her hips and cleared her throat loudly, tapping her boot as she studied their bald spots and waited.

After a moment, they slowly lifted their graying heads, doing a horribly bad job of looking surprised to see her. *Oh, brother,* she thought, hiding her smile.

"Haley Bell, darlin'!" Applegate exclaimed and Stanley echoed his greeting.

"Helllooo, fellas. Mind if I join you?"

Applegate stood and stole a chair from the table behind him. "Sure, sure. Sa-*ammm,*" he yelled. "Haley Bell needs a sweet tea! And a hamburger. You want a hamburger? Yeah, a hamburger," he bellowed when she nodded.

By now Haley was almost in stitches. "My car wouldn't start this morning. Imagine that?" she said. "And I was a little hurt that you didn't hang around this morning to tell me goodbye. It's almost lunchtime now. I mean, you did remember that I was leaving this morning, first thing. Right?"

"Of course I remembered. But why would I want to hang around just to watch you drive off?"

Haley's heart wrenched with love for her ornery grandpa.

"Yeah, Haley Bell, Applegate ain't getting any younger. Watching you drive off mighta been more'n his ol' heart could stand. Did you ever thank about that? He might just drop in yer tracks watchin' you drive off. Jest fall flat out in yer dust and that'd be it."

"I get the picture, Stanley," Haley chuckled. They were sure amping up the pity party. Laying a hand on Applegate's, she leaned in and kissed his washboard cheek. "Not that I think you're leaving me anytime soon, but I did some thinking and praying about the driving off and leaving you behind bit."

"What's going on over here?" Sam said, setting an amber glass of tea in front of her. "Applegate, you cause more ruckus than yer worth, disturbing my customers like that." He glared at her grandpa and smiled at her. "Your burger's comin up in a minute. I tossed the beef on the grill. Now, what's going on?"

Haley glanced around the table, clasped her hands together and smiled, confident this was the right thing to do. "Grandpa, what would you think about me moving home to Mule Hollow?"

For a second everything was stone-cold silent.

"Did you say, 'movin home'?" Applegate asked, his eyes brightening.

Haley nodded.

"Sam, did ya hear that? My Haley's moving home. Stanley, did ya hear?"

Haley laughed when she was suddenly engulfed in a bear hug. And it hit her that she'd just made the right decision. It might be complicated for her and a little bit hard, but it was right. She felt it deep inside.

Sam's wrinkles stretched to their limits, his grin was so big. "Well, Haley, it's about time you came to yor senses and come back where you belong."

Stanley slapped his hands together and grinned. "I think this calls for apple pie all around. What'd y'all thank about that?"

Haley grinned. "Stanley, I *thank* you're right. Sam, bring on the pie."

The news traveled fast that Haley Bell Thornton was here to stay. By the time the evening came around and she entered the community center to paint props, Haley figured everyone had heard. Including Will.

She'd had a busy afternoon, and while her head was spinning from the response she'd received from everyone in Mule Hollow, her ears were still burning from what Sugar had had to say about the news.

It had not been pretty.

But Haley felt a mixture of excitement, relief and trepidation about the entire idea. Of course, as she'd stressed to Sugar, it was all good. It was all going to work out great because Haley had a plan.

A plan she'd discussed with Lacy after praying about it. A plan that Lacy assured her was no accident. Lacy looked straight at her and told her that she felt confident that God had prepared her for this very moment all of her life…Haley still wasn't as convinced of that as Lacy, but she drew strength from Lacy's conviction.

That conviction meant nothing to Sugar.

"You're going to do what?" Sugar had screeched. Haley had expected nothing less from her assistant and friend.

"I'm going to open a real-estate office here. And I think I'm going to try my hand at flipping a couple of houses. There's really a need for someone to rehab some of the places on the market here."

"Haley, you have a job. You have a big fish waiting on you right this very moment to come back here and sell him a property. May I remind you that Marcus Sims has almost driven me crazy trying to find out where you are?"

"Sugar, I have to do this. I have to find something that matters to me on a level separate from ambition, money or even love. I have to find something in my life that surpasses all of that. And I think despite everything that's happened, it's here. Mule Hollow is where my roots are…and this is where I feel alive."

Sugar heaved a sigh. "I have to admit, you do sound, well, I can't really say you sound happy, but you sound different. I just hope this isn't some spur-of-the-moment thing and you wake up after you've made the break and regret what you're giving up."

Regret. Haley had chuckled over that six-letter word. If Sugar only knew.

Of course, as Haley stood outside the community center and prepared to enter it, she understood that for now she was running on adrenaline. She just prayed that tomorrow she didn't wake up and agree with Sugar. After all, she had a life in Beverly Hills. It wasn't making her happy; it wasn't fulfilling her the way she'd always thought it would. And though her head hadn't acknowledged it, she'd known in her heart for a while that she was heading down a long road that led nowhere emotionally. She'd been growing depressed and almost desperate for months now that she looked back on it. Maybe that was why she'd turned her car in the direction of Mule Hollow when she'd left Linc. She'd felt as if her world were crashing in around her and she couldn't scramble fast enough to keep her head up any longer.

Now she was getting the chance to find answers and at least make Applegate happy. Why, in just the hours since telling him her plan, he'd been beaming like the sun itself. And that made Haley very happy.

Feeling excited and edgy at the same time, Haley had decided to get a head start on some of the final painting that needed to be done on the props. Time was running out. With just six days left until dress rehearsal, everything needed to be finished.

She slipped inside the community center, smiling because, like Applegate and his front door, no one saw any need to lock the doors of the center. Mule Hollow—there just was no other place quite like it.

Walking toward the paint, she searched out the can of green, grabbed a brush from the drain in the kitchen, then went to work. It was just small stuff that needed attention, like rescuing three more trees that looked like Popsicles, so Haley set to work ruffling them up a bit. Overall, everything was looking great. Haley had a good feeling about the entire production. The room was quiet as she popped the top off two different types of green paint and set to work making the blocks into willowy trees.

Soon, if they didn't already, everyone would know that she was moving home to Mule Hollow. Word traveled like a grass fire in the small town. Of course, she knew that she was thinking about Will. She wondered what he would say when he found out that she'd made such a dramatic decision. The work would help settle her nerves.

She felt sure he hadn't expected so much when he'd promised to stay out of her way if she stayed until Christmas.

Just how well would he keep that promise now that she was staying indefinitely?

More important and worrisome—how well did she want him to? She might have made a huge life change, but she wasn't quite to the point where she could think about Will.

She knew there would be occasions when they'd have to be around each other. Like she'd thought earlier, just as long as they didn't have to be alone together.

That meant absolutely no more wild berry chases or gator hunts. Or pig traps.

Had she really experienced all of that in the few weeks since she'd been here? And all with Will.

Shaking her head at the irony of it, she studied the tree that was starting to actually look like a tree and made an adjustment to a fresh leafy ruffle, took a deep breath and continued painting. She enjoyed painting and had a natural talent for it, though she'd never kidded herself that it would be a talent that would have ever made her a living. But it was good for times like this, and she figured that if she ever did actually marry and have children, it would come in handy when it came to school projects. She hadn't thought about children in a long time. That was another of those regrets.

She hadn't had time to think about children. She'd been so busy making something of herself…. But she wanted children— at least she had before she'd started obsessing about succeeding at something other than being cute. She'd been thinking about kids a lot over the last year. She knew deep down that was part of the reason she'd agreed to marry Lincoln. Her biological clock was ticking. But before it was too late, she'd realized that it was also one of the many wrong reasons for marrying a man she didn't love. Of course, when she'd agreed to marry Darin that had been a mistake from the get-go. Her head and heart had been so messed up then, that children hadn't been a thought…. That had been Will's fault.

He'd doomed all of her relationships and yet, in her heart of hearts despite all the anger and the hurt and the confusion, when she thought about kids, she thought about Will.

The man made her nuts. Here she was thinking about him again. For a minute, she panicked. She was making a mistake coming back here. She couldn't face these ricocheting feelings. *Stop it, Haley.*

Applegate really needed her; family meant something. If she ran this time, she would never be able to face herself…or God. She had to stop running. She had to.

She was going to do this. She was committed to it. It was the first real commitment she'd made in years.

Peace came over her with the commitment. She was ready for a slower pace. She needed a slower pace. Maybe that was what had brought her back here in the first place. Maybe God knew all along that she needed to slow down, but she didn't know how to get off the merry-go-round.

In the silence of the room, Haley bowed her head. Right there in the middle of the Mule Hollow community center—all three thousand square feet of it—she thanked the Lord for leading her home. For not giving up on her.

Deciding the tree limb needed a bit of help, too, she hopped up and went in search for some brown paint. She had just picked the can up when she heard the door open.

"Haley."

Holding the can of paint like a shield, she swung around to find Will standing just inside the door. He didn't look happy to see her. And she knew she wasn't happy to see him, despite the ruckus her insides kicked up the instant he said her name.

Despite the peace she'd just felt, she wasn't ready to face him.

"Will," she managed to say, trying to hide her shock. "What are you doing here?"

He looked uncomfortable, too. "I needed to make some adjustments to the tracks. I didn't see your car."

Haley wiped a strand of hair out of her face with the back of her hand. "I rode with Applegate. He's down at the manger scene."

"Oh, yeah, I saw him down there."

Haley could tell he was uneasy. He'd come to avoid her and she'd messed up his plans.

"Look, this is silly. Don't let me stop you. I'm just doing a little last-minute work on the trees." She waved the can of paint—as if the man couldn't see the massive can already.

Will hooked the thumb of his left hand through a belt loop. "Nate struck again. Those definitely needed some help."

"That's what they're getting," she quipped, shooting him a tight smile. *Uncomfortable* was not even close to expressing the vibe passing between them. "So, I guess you heard?"

He rocked on his boot heel. "Yeah. Got a call a few hours ago."

"It made Applegate really happy."

"I'm sure it did. Look, I hope you're making the right decision. I hope I didn't influence you to do something you're going to regret."

Regret. "Will, believe it or not, we may have our differences, but you helped me make the right choice."

They stared at each other for a moment. "Look, I'm going to come back later to do this."

He turned to go, and Haley realized he was leaving. "Will, this is ridiculous. I'm not going to be bothered by you working over there."

He hesitated before striding to the stage. Haley's fingers tightened around the can as she spun away to stare unseeingly at the painting. She would get used to this.

Eventually, she and Will would be able to be around each other and not feel totally and utterly at odds. They would.

But it would take time. Time to forget the kiss—okay, so she hadn't meant to think about that kiss. But after all, it had only been roughly twenty-four hours since it had happened.

Twenty-four hours—was that all? Haley hesitated, caught up in the thought of the kiss. Oh yes, no way around it. It would positively take more than a mere twenty-four hours to forget Will's kiss.

But she could do it.

Would do it.

All she had to do was refocus on her plan. Which she had, and that was a good thing. She'd focus on moving, picking the property she wanted to purchase for renovating and selling, and on spending plenty of time with Applegate while adjusting to a better quality of life. Everything else would fall into place. She was certain that with plenty of prayer to keep her focused, she could handle being around Will. Just as long as they had limited alone time and no more wild berry chases or gator hunts.

Kisses were most assuredly out of the question.

But she knew the truth now. She paused with her brush hanging on the edge of the paint can and glanced at Will as he worked with his back to her. The truth was that no matter how many times her thoughts went back to the feel of Will's arms around her and the touch of his lips on hers, no matter how much she'd longed for him to love her despite the effect he had on her, she couldn't shake his betrayal and the grudge that remained because of it. The knowledge shook her and made her incredibly sad.

They'd been young and both made mistakes. She knew it was the truth. Still, she was having trouble accepting this. Prayer was a starting place. She had to trust that God would work everything out. She also had to take a long hard look at herself. Was she to blame? Had she been young and selfish? Remembering things like she'd wanted to remember them?

Chapter Twenty

Will stayed away for the three days after running into Haley in the community center. He hadn't meant for that to happen.

Three long days where he woke at daybreak and fell into bed well after it grew dark. The work was the only thing that kept him from going into town and making a fool of himself, but thankfully he had a deadline to meet and that was his saving grace.

When he'd gone to Applegate's to talk to Haley, he hadn't told her all of it. He'd almost told her that he still loved her. But he'd realized it wasn't time. That she wasn't ready to hear it from him.

But he knew it.

He loved her. He'd never stopped loving her.

He wanted her to be his. He'd always

wanted it, and though he'd been angry at her for years, despite everything, he still loved her. Even before realizing he'd been to blame for driving her away.

Now he'd been given the time he needed to convince her she loved him, too.

He just had to go about it patiently.

During the last three days, it hadn't been hard to keep up with what she was doing. His normally quiet workshop, where usually he could work without much interruption, had suddenly become Grand Central Station. The first day, Norma Sue, Esther Mae and Adela had stopped in. They'd come to thank him for his help with the production and to make certain that he planned to attend. While they'd been inviting him, they'd just *happened* to mention that Haley was keeping busy and would be helping with the dress rehearsal on Thursday night…and that he was on the props committee and though they knew he was busy, everyone, absolutely everyone was needed on the night of dress rehearsal and the two performance nights.

He thought they were very cute, and he was on to them one hundred percent. The little matchmakers were as busy as bees making honey trying to figure a way to get him and Haley together. He smiled thinking about it; he was happy to let them do their thing, as long as it was harmless. But he had to admit that so far they were right on target with all the couples they'd gotten together with their matchmaking.

But none of the couples had the kind of history that he and Haley shared, so he still wanted to be cautious.

The following day he had a visit from Applegate and Stanley. They came to tell him that whatever he'd done to keep Haley in town had worked. Applegate gave him one of his rare smiles that were starting to be seen more often than not, and it did Will's heart good to see it. It also reinforced what he'd felt was true—that Haley needed to be here, in Mule Hollow near Applegate.

Seeing App's happiness once more strengthened Will's resolve to keep his promise. If it took him staying out of Haley's way in order for her to come home and make her granddad happy, he would.

Even if it killed him.

And one day, when the time was right, and God was smiling on him, Will would get the desire of his heart.

Until then, he thought about her while he

worked. Saw her smile up at him from the swing on Thanksgiving Day. Saw her looking up at him in bewilderment from behind the bars of the pig trap. Saw her madder than a hornet, covered in mud, glaring at him after he'd kissed her. And he saw her standing above him in the hayloft, pitchfork in hand, the sweet morning sun illuminating her from the open door. He saw it all, but what stood out to him was her spirit in all the situations. She was vulnerable, yet she was strong. She'd fought against the odds to become the woman she was today. And he admired her and loved her more because of it.

He'd been such a fool, but now he knew there was no other woman for him. And if it took a lifetime, he'd prove to Haley that they were meant to be together. He may have let her down once, but he would find a way to prove to her that he would never do it again.

On Thursday afternoon he watched the freight truck pull away with his shipment, and he had never been so happy to see an order go out as he was to see that one leave. He was bone-weary from all the late nights and early mornings, but there was something to be said for not being able to sleep. It got things accomplished. Tonight he had the dress rehearsal…and he had to be there.

It was required. Glory, glory. Promise or no promise, he had a free pass for the next three nights.

Turning toward his house he practically Texas two-stepped his way up the walk.

It was time to see Haley.

When Haley walked out of her bedroom ready to head to town for dinner at Sam's, then on to the dress rehearsal, she'd expected her impatient grandfather to herd her out the door to the truck as he usually did. She wasn't expecting to find him holding out a chair for her at the kitchen table.

"What's going on, Grandpa?" she asked as she sank into the chair and watched him start to pace. He looked so fierce and pensive at the same time.

"Haley Bell, it's time fer me to come clean. You know, with you and Will's anniversary comin' up and all, time is running out."

She looked at him sharply. "We don't have an anniversary—"

He frowned. "Yep, darlin', you do. It ain't the one you should be havin' but the fact remains that you two share an anniversary whether ya want to admit it or not. And I gotta be straight, youngin, I still believe in my heart that when you ran off from y'all's wedding ten years ago come tomorrow, you made the mistake of yor life."

"Grandpa—"

His lifted eyebrow halted her denial. "I said then that you run off from the man you was s'posed to marry. And you been running ever since. Nope, don't deny it. You've been running ever since. That's what I said then and it bears repeating. Especially now after proving it by standin' up these other two fellas. And I figure that it's about time you stopped. That's why I come up with this here plan, this covert operation…. Only I didn't figure you to be so hardheaded."

"I'm hardheaded for reasons, Granddad," she said, feeling defensive despite the fact that she'd started to have a change of heart.

"Not none that make a bit a sense to me. Just because a man wanted to take care of you, cherish you, and try ta keep you safe like the good Lord instructs him to…it just ain't right that ya hold that against him fer the rest of his life."

His lips drooped deeper, his eyes narrowing. Haley crossed her arms defensively, even though she'd been at war with herself over these very thoughts.

"That boy ain't never told you why he decided to live here, has he?"

Not completely. Haley shook her head. She was getting a headache and she lifted her fingers to massage her temple. She'd never asked him and he'd never offered any explanation.

Applegate hung his head in disgust. "I tell ya. For two smart people, a body lookin' in who didn't know any better would thank the two of you were a few pegs short of a book—"

Haley stood and hushed him with an impulsive hug as much for him as for her. She knew he only wanted what was best for her. But he couldn't help her on this. Couldn't he see that? Still, the fact that he'd come up with a covert operation to get her and Will together again touched her. It was just so Applegate…at least the Applegate she'd started seeing for the first time since arriving home. The newly romantic-at-heart Applegate—the man her grandma Birdie must have always seen.

Squeezing him hard, she kissed his cheek.

"Thank you, Grandpa. But, wrong or right, you can't do this for me. No one can. I have to fuddle my way through all of this on my own. No," she amended. "I take that back. You can pray that God will lead me."

An hour later she walked out of Sam's. Still fuddled and feeling restless, she'd excused herself ahead of the crowd. Outside, bowing her head against a blast of cold air, she'd only walked a few steps when she heard someone call Will's name. She looked up to see Ashby Templeton, the owner of the dress store, waving at Will as he stepped from his truck.

Irrationally panicked, Haley practically dove off the sidewalk to hide behind a truck so that Will wouldn't see her. It was the silliest thing in the world for her to do. But after not seeing him for three days and suddenly to be confronted with him like this, she reacted all…Haley Bell-ish!

She enhanced the image further when she peeked around the edge of the truck cab to watch him.

"Will," Ashby called. "Could you help me for a minute?"

The smile he gave Ashby curled Haley's

toes, and as he strode purposefully across the street toward the willowy brunette, Haley felt a stab of jealousy slash through her. When he laughed at something she said as he stepped up onto the sidewalk beside her, Haley felt sick. It was worse when they disappeared into the dress store, and Haley wanted to follow them.

Jealousy—the very idea irked Haley. Will Sutton could help every single woman who lived or came to visit Mule Hollow, and it shouldn't matter to her. Not in the least. After all, they were done. Weren't they?

The sound of an approaching truck reminded Haley that she needed to move on. She certainly didn't want anyone to see her hiding between trucks and start a new Haley Bell story, so she stepped back onto the sidewalk and hurried toward the community center. Berating herself all the way. Really, what did it matter to her if Will had been beaming like a lantern when Ashby had called his name? If there was no future for them, then she should be prepared for someone else to make a play for Will's heart. The idea didn't sit well with her. Still, as she let herself into the building, she reluctantly glanced back across the street. He was still inside the store. What could he be doing?

Pushing the question away, she went to the kitchen to put on a pot of coffee. Since everyone would be working late, she knew coffee would be needed. She needed it. She saw that Dottie or one of the ladies from the Sweet Shop had dropped off a pan of brownies and some fudge as a treat for everyone. Haley thought that was really nice since they were working overtime trying to get enough stock made up to sell over the next two days. Haley opened the cabinet and pulled out the coffee canister and filter. Within moments she had the coffee brewing, but her attempt to distract herself with the task didn't do the job. The tickle at the back of her mind was hard to ignore. What was he doing over there at Ashby's?

Unable to stand it any longer, she stomped to the large front window and peered out like a nosy neighbor. She saw immediately that dinner was over at Sam's and there was a stampede of people coming down the sidewalk to report for dress rehearsal.

She also noted that neither Ashby nor Will were part of the group.

Seized by an irrational wave of guilt,

despite no one knowing she'd been spying on Will, she spun from the window. Searching for something to do, she grabbed up a table-cloth and unfurled it over a table just as the doors flew open. People flooded inside in a rush of laughter and jokes.

It was a loud few moments of hustle and flow as people separated into their places for the night. All those with parts headed to the back of the building to the dressing rooms where they would change into their costumes for the first time. Adela went with the cast, since she was in charge of fitting and altering costumes. To Haley's dismay, Esther Mae hurried over to help her.

"I thought you were helping with costumes?" Haley said, trying not to sound too hopeful. Her head was too full of the sudden idea that if she wasn't careful, she might lose Will forever.

Esther shook her head. "Adela will call me if she needs me."

Haley nodded, her attention snagged on Molly as her dark-headed husband, Bob, gave her a quick kiss. Haley watched the way they looked at each other before he headed to the back to change. As if not wanting to be away from her too long, he teasingly tugged on one of her dark curls before striding toward the dressing rooms. It was a sweet, endearing exchange that suddenly caused a lump to form in Haley's throat. Overwhelmed with sentiment, she busied herself with smoothing out the tablecloth, her thoughts swinging to Will. She was filled with a sense of urgency that she didn't want to feel. She'd been praying and asking the Lord to guide her, *calmly.* She didn't want to fall into her old pattern of making overly emotional decisions. Easier said than done when thoughts of the man hounded her. Again.

Everything made her think of him. As if he'd heard her, he slipped into the building a moment later, tall, breathtakingly handsome and smiling down at Ashby. He was carrying a box, and they looked so much like one of the other couples that Haley lost her breath.

"They are the cutest couple," Esther Mae sighed. "They remind me of me and my Hank twenty years ago."

Haley shot a glare at the older woman, only then realizing Esther Mae was watching Molly and Bob, referring to them, not Will and Ashby. Haley should have felt relieved—

well, technically she shouldn't have been feeling anything. But that was moot at this point because she was startled by the sheer force of emotion raging through her. Even her hands trembled.

Thank goodness no one beside her seemed to notice her dilemma. Norma Sue's appearance that instant was a blessing.

"Everything reminds you of you and Hank," she said in a hushed whisper coming down the aisle from the dressing room. "Now, what's up, Haley? We figure things must be going pretty good between you and Will, you know with you moving back and all," she said, looking at Haley expectantly.

So much for thinking she was going to swing through the night untouched. Haley picked up another tablecloth and held on to it like a shield. "Don't get your hopes up. I've sworn off men for at least a year. And Will Sutton for life!" Where had that come from?

"A year?" Esther Mae shrieked, immediately drawing looks from everyone as she made a beeline around the edge of the table to hover beside Norma Sue, who was looking flabbergasted herself.

"Did you say a year?" she grunted disbelieving. "Where in the world did that come from?"

Haley felt a little put out, especially since the words had just popped out of her mouth. She'd been just as surprised to hear the news as they had, but now that she thought about it, maybe it was for the best. She needed to get her head on straight before she thought about moving forward romantically with anyone. Particularly if she were going to make sensible decisions and give the Lord a chance to guide her.

"Yes. A year," she said forcefully. "And I just decided it this minute." It wouldn't be the first time she'd made a spur-of-the-moment decision, and she'd come to realize that it probably wouldn't be her last. But this at least sounded like the right choice, despite her heart telling her she was a fool.

"And no Will?" Esther Mae whispered, a hand coming up to rest against her cheek.

Haley nodded emphatically. No Will. Absolutely!

"Well, this will not do. Not do at all," Esther Mae said, fanning herself with her hands, her brow furrowed.

Norma Sue patted her friend's arm. "Now, calm down, Esther Mae. It's just time. Time changes everything."

"Time," Ester wailed, then ducked her chin in an effort to be inconspicuous.

Too late for that—everyone was watching them. Including Will and her frowning grandpa. Haley got a lump in her stomach that knotted up and burned like fire. She was probably getting an ulcer. She was realizing that coming back to Mule Hollow was going to be harder than she thought. Spinning away from Will's observant eyes, she attacked the slightly wrinkled tablecloth with a vengeance, feeling more foolish and lost than ever. Wasn't trusting the Lord supposed to make things better? Norma Sue and Esther Mae jumped into the fray, smoothing wrinkles down the long table.

"Haley, obviously you haven't noticed how Will looks at you when you aren't looking at him," Esther Mae said, almost breathless from the fast pace they were all working at in their wrinkle smoothing. "Why, the man gazes at you so wistfully that it makes my heart go pitter-patter."

"It doesn't matter to me how he looks at me," she snapped, while her heart did a little of its own pitter-pattering thinking about Will watching her wistfully. She pushed the idea away.

Lacy called all actors to the stage—which meant that Norma Sue would at least have to give up her harassment for the moment. She gave Haley a come-on-get-yourself-together-girl look before she headed off to join the cast. When Esther Mae started to speak, Haley beat her to it, needing space to try and clear her head. "I'm going to go get some supplies from the back, Esther Mae." Her hands were shaking as she hurried toward the back. Halfway there she had to pass by Will, and despite everything, her eyes were drawn to him. He was watching her, too, with somber dark eyes. She wished she'd kept her eyes to herself as she tore her gaze away and quickened her steps.

The storeroom was past the kitchen on the opposite side of the big room from the dressing rooms, so it was a safe place to go for some much-needed peace. Almost in panic mode, she would have kept walking straight out the back door, which was directly to the back of the storeroom, if she'd had her car waiting. But she'd ridden in with Applegate, saving her from an easy escape. Still, as she slumped against the wall, it was all she could do not to run. Reeling, she slid down to sit on the top of the metal trash can squeezed between a wall of wide shelves and a row of cabinets. With only the mop and broom to see her, she dropped her forehead into her hands. *What was she doing?*

Maybe Sugar was right. Maybe this wasn't such a good idea after all.

No.

She was a big girl, and despite the convoluted feelings that seemed to be stopping up her lines of communication between her head and her heart, Haley knew moving home was the right thing to do. If she could just make it through the holidays, then it would be easier. After all, the holidays were hard on her every year. No matter where she was and despite having denied it to Applegate, it had everything to do with tomorrow.

The day that would have been her wedding anniversary if she'd married Will ten years ago.

"Haley."

The sound of Will's voice sent ripples of unwanted happiness coursing through her. He stepped around the doorway and blocked her exit, filling the room with his presence.

"What do you want?" The words sounded harsher than she'd meant them to. "You said you would stay out of my way." He couldn't know how much she needed to keep distance between them.

"Everyone giving you a hard time?"

He'd read between the lines and she shot him a disgruntled look that said it all. How could she find her own way with so many trying to give her directions?

"It will get better, Haley."

Easy for him to say. She rammed her hands though her hair and closed her eyes. "I hope so," she sighed, wishing he would leave. Needing him to leave.

After a moment of silence, she got her wish and, though her eyes were closed, she felt him turn to go.

Her eyes flew open. "Wait." The word tore from her, stopping him. He turned slowly. "Why did you do it? Why did you move away after you were going to make me stay?" She didn't have to elaborate. He knew what she wanted to know. What she needed to know.

His expressive brown eyes softened. "Because running isn't something unique to you, Haley. I may have tried to keep you here out of a misguided effort to love and protect you but..." He paused, his beautiful voice drifting away as his gaze sharpened with emotion that tore at her defenses. "After you left there was nothing for me here. And everywhere I looked I saw you. I couldn't take that day in and day out."

"Then why did you come back?" She pulled her eyes away from his gaze and studied her tightly clasped hands.

"I didn't realize it then but I think a part of me was hoping you would come home. I came back for you, Haley."

Chapter Twenty-One

The play went well on Friday night. The house was packed. Women were everywhere. After all, Mule Hollow was the little town that advertised for wives. It was the little town that Lacy Brown had painted the colors of the rainbow and Molly Popp wrote about in her weekly newspaper column, and it was the place a bunch of women hoped to find their one, true love.

Yeah, right, Will thought sullenly. He'd hoped for the same thing. And he'd found it, but so far, it hadn't done him a bit of good.

Tonight he watched from behind the scenes, literally, as he and Applegate took care of changing the scenes between acts. He watched the play on autopilot, his thoughts with Haley instead. After his revelation to her the night before, she had looked at him with such disgust that he'd left her there. After all, he'd promised her he'd stay away from her. For the rest of the night they'd kept their distance and, despite Applegate's hounding that he needed to do something, Will went home from rehearsal feeling like his world was once again crashing in around him.

His commitment to the show and a long talk with the Lord had helped him make the drive into town tonight for the opening night of the production. Even Applegate was quiet as they managed the scene changes together. Both of them knew that it should have been Will's ten-year anniversary. Until last night when she'd looked at him with such disdain, he'd held hopes that today would be different. That today might have dawned with hope in it for a new beginning. The reality was that any future for them looked bleak.

When the play was over and the lights went out, Will escaped to his truck with every intention of disappearing for the remainder of the night. The play had gone well. The attendance was staggering, and the remainder of the evening promised to be a festive celebration.

All the more reason for him to leave. He was getting into his truck when Clint stopped him.

"Buddy, are you okay?"

"Hey, Clint." Will glanced at his friend. They were alone since everyone was already down at Sam's for cookies and punch. "Honestly, I'm not doing okay. I'm tired, Clint. It seems like I've been trying my whole life to build a life. But it boils down to this—if Haley isn't going to share it with me then I'm just spinning my wheels. I know that and am at a loss as to what to do."

Clint studied him. "Every relationship has obstacles to overcome, Will. Admittedly, the two of you have a hard history to overcome, but it can be done. It's going to take time."

Will gave a caustic grunt. Time. He felt like he'd wasted half his life and time was running out.

"Trust the Lord, Will. It might not seem like it, but He's got your back."

Will studied the dark sky. He knew it was true. That God hadn't forsaken him. He knew in his heart that if it was His will, anything was possible. Even Haley being able to forgive him. If she could ever do that then maybe she could love him again. But it was the *maybe* that pained him.

"So, why are you leaving?" Clint asked.

"I'm not feeling very sociable. And I promised her I'd stay out of her way if she moved back to Mule Hollow."

Clint looked at him as if he were loco. "Well, why would you want to do something like that?"

"Desperate, I guess. Only thing I could think of to keep her from running off again." Will started the engine of his truck and shifted to Reverse.

Grinning, Clint stepped away from the truck. "Sounds to me like you need to come up with another plan."

Will drove off wishing someone would give him a better plan because at the moment he was all out of ideas.

The production had gone well Friday night. Haley had purposefully taken her car to town in case she'd needed to leave. Not run, but leave to go back to Applegate's. She'd committed to not running and she wasn't no matter what.

She'd helped Adela take tickets at the door and thus hadn't needed to have any contact with Will, though she'd found herself watching him in the shadows for most of the evening. He'd looked grim the entire night. His eyes, troubled, almost pained.

The look cut Haley as nothing else had. He was hurting and it was plain to see. But at the rehearsal when he'd said he'd come back for her, she hadn't said anything. She'd been afraid to trust the emotions his words stirred within her. Watching him on Friday night, still unable to understand the emotions bashing around inside of her, she left as soon as the program was over.

By Saturday morning she was a wreck. She'd had a hard night and the day didn't get any better. Her emotions were so raw and conflicting that she spent most of it out riding her horse. Hiding out from Applegate and also needing to distance herself from the pain she'd seen in Will's eyes. The pain, which just a few weeks ago would have made her feel vindicated, but today made her feel empty.

She arrived at the second and final presentation knowing something had to change, because she couldn't continue with turmoil. She prayed for God to lead her.

When Will didn't show up for the final

performance, she found it hard to concentrate on anything except worrying about where he was.

She'd hoped to see him, had wanted him to be there.

The realization came as she watched Molly and Bob portraying Mary and Joseph in the play. Haley was suddenly struck by the bond that built between them as they shared in the extraordinary experience that God had chosen them for. Though they faced much trial and tribulation along the nine-month journey to Jesus's birth, God had blessed them with His love, strength and faith that they were the chosen couple. He'd also blessed them with each other's strength.

It was touching to witness it, and realize that Mary and Joseph were real people caught up in extraordinary events together.

When the play was over, Haley was lost in the crowd and in thought as she trailed behind the group to the bonfire. As everyone began to sing Christmas carols, all songs she loved, she couldn't join in. Her heart wasn't in it. The sadness that had been following her caught up with her.

She wanted to share her life with someone. All she could think of was that Will wasn't beside her. Did she really need time to figure out what she wanted out of life?

Because she was holding on to a silly grudge.

She slipped from the crowd and walked over to the Nativity scene. Christmas was almost here. The celebration of Jesus' birth. A time of great joy.

A time of renewing, of remembering what was important.

She knew what was important, but could she trust herself? A tear slipped down her cheek and Haley brushed it away with the back of her hand. She looked hard into her heart and didn't like what she saw. God had given her something that not everyone got to experience in their lifetime, and she'd selfishly thrown it away and blamed her problems on everyone but herself. She'd tossed everything aside without seeking His guidance and will in her life. And still, with all of His infinite love, He'd brought her back to Mule Hollow and given her a second chance—

"Haley."

At the sound of her name on Will's voice, she spun around. "Will." Her heart and head began pounding out a duet.

"Haley, I have something to say."

She took a step toward him, overwhelmed by the timing and the clarity that suddenly suffused her being. "I have something to say, too. I—where have you been?"

"Thinking. Praying. Coming to my senses."

Haley took another quick step toward him. He looked so wonderful, obviously having dressed for the evening, though he had only just now shown up. "Me, too."

"I know I promised to stay away from you. But I've come to tell you that I'm going to have to break my promise."

Haley smiled. Her heart was about to bust out of her chest. He looked so serious. His brown eyes caught just a hint of the flames from the fire down the street. "You are?" she managed to say.

"Yes. I should have come for you before, when you ran. I shouldn't have let you go. Not without a fight. Even though I thought I wasn't what you wanted, I should have at least fought to keep you. No wonder you can't forgive me."

"I do forgive you. But only if you can forgive me."

"What?"

Haley laughed and closed the gap between them in one stride, the chains of the past falling away. "We both messed up. And I was just standing here, thinking about how God has given us another chance to have a life together and because I had some puny little grudge I was going to let you get away from me because I couldn't trust my feelings."

Will frowned. "After the way I behaved that's understandable. But…" He reached out and cupped her face in his hands and looked deep into her eyes. "But, I make this promise to you here and now, I let you down once. I didn't put your wants and needs on the same level as mine and that will never happen again."

"Will," Haley murmured, reveling in the feel of his warm palms against her cheeks and the look of love in his eyes.

"I love you, Haley. I don't want to waste another moment without you."

Haley knew it was true. They'd both made mistakes and that they would work them out. Later. But right now, there was only one thing she wanted. "Will," she said again.

"What?" he asked, looking so serious that Haley couldn't help but smile.

"I love you, too," she chuckled, then added, as the light brightened in his beautiful eyes, "now, could you put me out of my misery and kiss me please? I don't want to waste another minute."

His eyes crinkled at the edges as a smile bloomed across his face and lifted into his eyes. "You don't have to ask me twice," he murmured.

The low, husky sound of his words sent joy straight through Haley's heart and she knew as long as she lived, she would never take this love for granted again.

"I love you, Haley Bell," Will said, then he lowered his lips to hers and kissed her as though he meant it.

And this time Haley believed him.

Epilogue

"Are you ready?" Applegate asked, looking down at Haley, his expression grim, his nervousness surprising her. She smiled up at her sweet granddad, the commander of "Operation: Married by Christmas." She loved it! Just the thought that he loved her enough to bring her and Will together again tickled her soul.

"Well, don't just stand there," Norma Sue hissed from where she and Esther Mae were hiding behind the door. They were her wedding planners, which was fitting since they, too, had been part of the covert operation to get her married.

"And don't even think—" Esther Mae added, stepping in front of the church exit "—about coming back this way until it's as Mrs. Will Sutton! 'Cause me and Norma might be in our sixties, but we'll tackle you and hold you down this time."

Haley chuckled. "Believe me, this time someone would have to drag me away from that altar," she whispered with a wink. Then she looked up at Applegate and nodded.

She'd floated through Christmas on a cloud of happiness. Not taking anything for granted, she'd never felt so blessed in all of her life. But she'd known that the entire town worried as they helped her plan her wedding, knowing her history and that she might choose at any given moment to run. But minutes before as Adela had begun to play the "Wedding March," Norma Sue and Esther Mae had pulled the doors of the chapel open, and she'd seen Will standing at the altar waiting for her, Haley had had no worries. This was it, her happily ever after.

The congregation of friendly faces turned to watch her, and Haley's smile grew and her heart skipped with happiness as her granddad patted her hand. This was her family. The place she felt loved and safe. The place where she now knew all her dreams would come true.

Will was smiling as her gaze met his. She knew he was as ready as she was to begin their new life together.

"Let's go, Grandpa. I'm ready. I'm so ready."

Like a horse out of a starting gate, Applegate took off. Haley didn't think that there had ever been a wedding march that had been as fast. Within seconds she was being handed over to Will, and if she hadn't known better she'd have thought Applegate was trying to get rid of her. But one look into his wizened eyes told her that wasn't the case.

Pastor Allen spoke the vows, and Haley and Will managed to make it through the service, though Haley found herself giggling as she said her vows. She couldn't help it. She was feeling so joyful that she was bubbling inside. And Will, why he had tears in his eyes. Tears.

When the service ended, Pastor Allen said that Will could kiss the bride, and he did, and Haley just kept right on smiling….

She didn't think she would ever stop.

* * * * *

Dear Reader,

I'm so glad you've chosen to spend a few hours in Mule Hollow with me and the gang! I pray you chuckle and relax, but also that you'll be inspired while you're visiting my wacky little town of loveable matchmakers. I loved telling Haley and Will's story. They were able to overcome an unpleasant past by forgiving each other and choosing to move forward. There were many obstacles in their way, but at the root of all their problems was a lack of communication on a large scale between all involved, not only Haley and Will. Strong personal relationships revolve around good communication. Most importantly, that includes a relationship with God. I believe if you want to hear His voice then you need to keep the lines of communication open through prayer, studying His word and storing it in your heart. Haley let herself drift away while she let everything else in her life take over. It's easy to do, it has happened to me, but I am so thankful that, as He did with Haley, God calls us back to Himself.

Talk to God today, it's the best conversation you'll ever have!

I love hearing from readers—you can reach me through my Web site debraclopton.com, or my P.O. Box,1125, Madisonville, Texas 77864. I try to respond to everything…if I've missed you somehow I am sorry, but please know your letter was greatly appreciated.

Until next time, live, laugh and love God with all your hearts,

Debra Clopton

QUESTIONS FOR DISCUSSION

1. What did you think about this story? Did you enjoy it? What character did you enjoy the most? What scene? (I vote for the gator scene since it came from my very own up close and personal encounter with a Texas gator!)

2. On the deeper issues of this book what character did you relate to the most?

3. Do you think the people of Mule Hollow loved Haley Bell so much they were blind to how they were injuring her self-image? Do you think they did anything wrong? Or do you believe Haley shouldn't have taken it personally?

4. Like Haley, have you ever felt so misunderstood or overwhelmed by your circumstances that you were tempted to run away from your life? How did you deal with this?

5. How do you think Haley's overwhelming need to achieve her dreams related to her

lack of self-image? Do you believe she did what she had to do even though she hurt Will? Along those same lines, do you think it took an act of strength or cowardice to walk away before exchanging vows with Will? Do you think she needed to leave Mule Hollow to find her inner strength?

6. Do you think Haley's lack of self-worth would have ultimately hurt their chances of a happy, successful life if she'd stayed and gone through with the wedding? Why or why not?

7. Unfortunately, married people leave behind their families every day to go "find themselves." What are your views about this? What does the Bible have to say about this?

8. Ironically, Will's sudden decision to change the plans he and Haley had made together, and for them to remain in Mule Hollow, was his attempt at stepping up and protecting Haley from the harsh realities of the world. Biblically considered, is that

what a husband is supposed to do? Should he have discussed such a decision with Haley?

9. I enjoyed writing this book because despite the hard issues the characters were dealing with love was actually the driving force of everyone's actions. Misunderstanding and a breakdown in communication by all people involved was a major problem. How do these issues affect your relationships? Do you think building a stronger relationship with God, reading the Bible on a regular basis and praying daily could help people in their other relationships? Discuss what you think makes a successful marriage.

P.S. I hope you'll join me back in Mule Hollow in January 2008 with Next Door Daddy—this story is straight from my heart.

HEARTWARMING INSPIRATIONAL ROMANCE

Contemporary,
inspirational romances
with Christian characters
facing the challenges
of life and love
in today's world.

**NOW AVAILABLE IN REGULAR
AND LARGER-PRINT FORMATS.**

Steeple
Hill®

For exciting stories that reflect traditional values,
visit:
www.SteepleHill.com

Love Inspired ®
SUSPENSE
RIVETING INSPIRATIONAL ROMANCE

Watch for our new series of
edge-of-your-seat suspense novels.
These contemporary tales
of intrigue and romance
feature Christian characters
facing challenges to their faith...
and their lives!

**Steeple
Hill**®